Around the World in Under Eighty Days

DR CHETTIAR V LORD HARRIS TRILOGY: BOOK ONE

VELLINGIRI RAJA BADRAKALIMUTHU

INDIA • SINGAPORE • MALAYSIA

ISBN 979-8-89233-928-5

Other books by the Author

Kural (Tamil)

A Way With The Fairies

A Memory of Water

Inspired by Around The World in Eighty Days
by Jules Verne

To

Satyavathi who told me the story of how Murugan and Vinayakan raced around the world

Contents

Chapter One

21 June 1907

Day One

Lutz House, Madras

Dr Vellingiri Chettiar resided at Lutz House in Mylapore. This was in the British city of Madras, which was the administrative capital of the Madras Presidency. This luxurious mansion, surrounded by acres of forest, had been bought from a Portuguese man by Dr Chettiar's father. The senior Chettiar had started as a native translator for the Portuguese merchants and rose to become an eminent trader at Parry's economic hub of Madras. He could not but become wealthy as his enterprise had a modest yet fair share of 70% of foreign trade of which 32% was with the British. He was grateful to Lord Subramanya for his profit from importing cotton-piece goods, cotton twist and cotton yarn, metals and kerosene oil and exporting animal hides, skin, raw cotton, coffee, tea, and grain.

Amongst the 32 million population in the Presidency, of which fifteen million spoke Tamil, he was one of the select Hindustanis to have an account at Madras Bank that had been founded in 1863 with a capital of £100,000-pound sterling.

It was then renamed as the Bank of Madras as it merged with the Carnatic, Asiatic and the Bank of Madras banks. It was no surprise that he had bought Lutz House, which used to be part of the barracks for the Portuguese. As did his opulent belly, his critics inflated in time and accused him of trading patriotism for prosperity. His avarice alienated him even more from the people of Madras than when his wife died following labour. Many felt that their prayer to various deities, be they Saivaites, Vaishnavaites, Lingayats or tribes who worshipped relics of God made from a handful of turmeric, and even a good measure of Muslims and Christians were vindicated. The senior Chettiar though believed it was a call from Lord Subramanya that he make his son a doctor. The Madras Medical College established in 1835 in due course conferred a degree of medicine to his only son Vellingiri Chettiar. His mission accomplished, the senior Chettiar reached the eternal abode of Lord Subramanya.

Hence, Dr Chettiar inherited Lutz House. And, perhaps, that was the only thing he had inherited from the senior Chettiar. Dr Chettiar was a polymath. He held a Bachelor of Arts degree from the Presidency College. But for his impatience, he would have sat exams at the College of Engineering in Guindy. However, what he had learnt there had been useful when he'd modified Helmholtz's ophthalmoscope and added a concave mirror to make it handheld – it was a matter of trivial annoyance to his English patients who were unhappy that their private thoughts could be read whilst he peered deep into their retinas.

He smiled, knowing that he could infer a lot more from the moment they stepped into his wood-panelled clinic. The English ladies were more than willing for him not to use Laennec's stethoscope, for he was a tall, coffee-nut coloured man, virile from mastering *mal*, the art of wrestling and *silambam*. Whilst he listened for rhonchi and heart murmurs from rheumatic fever, they hoped that he would translate their heartbeat into one of the many languages that he spoke, Latin, French, Portuguese, Tamil, Telugu, Kannada, Malayalam, Hindi, Urdu, and Sanskrit.

Dr Chettiar was a hedonist and connoisseur of experiences that brought forth pleasure to his senses. He had listened to baroque compositions in Vienna and Prague and Carnatic music in the *sabhas* of Madras. He had read Homer and Kambar, the Vedas and *Thirukkural.*

And that morning when he woke up, on the marble floor of his bedroom, he could easily brush away pain from the still-raw bite marks, but the hangover from various fluids, including those exchanged through the act of sex, stung every cell in his brain. He pushed under his neck, the voluminous *Traite des Degenerescences* by Morel, which had propounded an understanding of mental illness upon the theory of degeneration and hyperextended his head as if it would help. As Director for Health, he was entrusted with the cholera-prevention programme, which was an illness that he held with such contempt due to personal reasons that it had a significant bearing on his character. We will understand more of this later.

He was a member of the governor's executive council created by Pitt's India Act of 1784, abolished by the Government of India Act of 1833 and restored by the Indian Council Act of 1861. He was rumoured to be an influential member of the Madras Native Association, the first anti-British political organisation established by Garzulu Lakshminarain Chetty. A rumour that he never denied. He crawled up to a selection of newspapers, including the Madras Times that had been left on the coffee table on the veranda that morning along with his herbal tea infused with willow bark that contained acetylsalicylate. It was then that Mr One Too-Many, his secretary, arrived to announce that a young, rounded stranger, wearing flowing kurta and dhoti, accompanied by a turban, a Mr Paneer Janardhana Pillai, had arrived.

He finally said, 'Mr Pillai was pleasing to behold.'

That seemed to be an incendiary that exploded in his head and he sat upright and pulled over a white dhoti that never assumed to clothe him.

'A duel has commenced between two arch enemies to see who can make it around the world fastest' wrote the conservative, unionist and imperialist *Times* that sold 140,000 copies at 3d per copy.

'Arch-rivals to race across the world,' headlined *The Daily Telegraph,* organ of the middle classes. *The Daily Telegraph* sold at 1d per copy and had sponsored HM Stanley's expedition to Africa.

'Indian challenges British Empire,' cried *The Hindu* published from Madras since 1880.

None of them mentioned the murder of Governor Roberts, not even the vernacular *Swadesimitran* published by Subramanya Iyer, who, Tamil not being his forte, had said, 'The shortcoming is in the language. It does not have a wealth of vocabulary in practical matters. Prose, as such, is not common in Tamil.' Perhaps murder was commonplace and, hence, inconsequential.

Dr Chettiar could now recall the events of the previous night at the Grand Ball in honour of His Majesty at the Madras Cricket Club.

The Previous Night, 20 June 1907

Amidst the fanfare at Madras Cricket Cub that hosted the Grand Ball in honour of His Majesty, Lord Harris – known for having scored centuries for Eton, Oxford, Kent, and England – stood to make an announcement. 'In honour of His Majesty, I have set myself a challenge to circumnavigate the world in less than eighty days and I am leaving tonight on this journey!'

Perhaps nothing more would have happened if Lord Harris had not stared, even if it was in passing, at Dr Chettiar during his announcement. Perhaps men should not have proclaimed, 'There is no one in this world who is brave enough to challenge Lord Harris.' Perhaps his eyes that searched for Miss Roberts should have succeeded, for it was to impress her that he had come up with such an audacious challenge.

The only reason for Dr Chettiar's presence there was in his formal position as a member of the governor's executive council, for natives were not allowed to become members of the Madras Cricket Club. Dr Chettiar stood up, maintaining a precarious balance between alcohol and blood rushing to his brain as did his feet balance will against gravity. That he had always been unhappy with exclusion from the Madras Cricket Club just because he was a native was an understatement. His stint for Madras Medical College as a batsman was legendary, and under his captaincy, he had walked his team out of Universities Cup final when his spinner was unfairly called for throwing. The cup was awarded to the opposite team but victory belonged to Dr Chettiar.

Nor were his exploits for Cambridge University at Lords easily forgotten. Cambridge needed to score twenty-nine to win. They were down to their last men. The Oxford team captain was prematurely celebrating victory. Dr Chettiar who had battled through the innings had to score as well as protect his eleventh man from facing the opposition's bowling. He took guard. The first ball was a hook. The second straight driven. The third was driven through the covers. The fourth pulled. The fifth ball carted off dancing down the pitch. Six. Six. Six. Six. Six. Dr Chettiar remained on ninety-nine not out. Hence, it was understandable why he was disappointed with the archaic rules of the Madras Cricket Club regarding membership. The only piece of information that should be mentioned was that on both those aforementioned events on the cricket pitch, the opposition teams were captained by none other than Lord Harris.

'Gentlemen.' He had to say that with his eyes closed, for there weren't that many subscribers to that title, and then he opened his eyes and said, 'Having defeated Lord Harris twice,' Lord Harris stood up to protest but Dr Chettiar continued, 'On and off the field, I challenge my dear friend, Lord Harris. I will race him around the world and make it a hat-trick of victories!'

'Impertinent!'

'Impossible!'

'Indian?'

And then Lord Harris landed a punch on Dr Chettiar's face that made Dr Chettiar fall.

Dr Chettiar rose up and treated the punch as if it was at its best, necessary medication against his intoxicated state and at worst, the exposure of Lord Harris's regressive psyche at that moment.

He continued, 'Not only will I accomplish this feat faster than Lord Harris but, from when I leave the shores of India until I present myself at Fort St George, Madras, I will not set foot on British soil through this journey nor use a British company for transport!'

Governor Roberts stood up. A short portly man, with a thick silver moustache, he appeared to be in haste to bring the proceedings to an end. And why wouldn't he? He had a rendezvous.

'Why, that will make the journey even more interesting for Lord Harris,' he said.

'And if I win,' Dr Chettiar continued firmly. 'I would want to be made a member of the Madras Cricket Club.'

'What?'

'No!'

'Never!'

The president of the Madras Cricket Club asked, 'And if you lose?'

'I will resign from the Executive Council and transfer all my shares of the Bank of Madras to Lord Harris,' he replied.

'On behalf of His Majesty, I approve of this duel!' the president of the Madras Cricket Club announced and raised a toast.

'Now, if you would excuse me, gentlemen, I have to wash my blood-stained face,' said Dr Chettiar, wiping his bleeding nose as he withdrew to the washroom followed by Lord Harris.

It was at that moment that the dare devil act of cannonball flight happened with a youthful native landing on the balcony of the Madras Cricket Club. Crowd roared.

Further to this, Governor Roberts was murdered in the washroom of the Madras Cricket Club.

The papers reported a gunshot being heard, a lady shrieking, Dr Chettiar walking out of the washroom to report that Governor Roberts had been shot dead, and Lord Harris informing people that a native man had escaped, carrying someone on his shoulder.

The articles in the papers ended with the General of the Madras regiment vowing that this native monkey who had murdered Governor Roberts would have nowhere to hide in the British Empire.

The Present Day – 21 June 1907, Day One

Mr Pillai bowed and stood obedient in front of Dr Chettiar as the latter became reacquainted with the events from the previous night.

'Tell me about yourself, Mr Pillai,' he said as he stood up, clutching his falling dhoti.

'I am from Ramanathapuram and I have completed the Pre-University Course. I am trained in *ottam tullal* and I can play the violin. I have received accolades for my *tanam.* I came to Madras to be part of the drama *sabhas.* When my attempts failed, I found a job as secretary to Mr Kuppusamy Naidoo and he said that I should speak to you as you are looking for a manager,' Mr Pillai said.

Dr Chettiar gazed at Mr Pillai. His ears were in admiration of the martial arts of which Mr Pillai claimed to be an exponent, yet they were in an argument with his eyes, which detected the lustrous grace that had been perhaps acquired from training in music and dance.

'Are you trained in *varmam*?'

'Yes,' Mr Pillai confirmed.

'Good. Pack your clothes and report back to my house in an hour. We have a journey ahead of us,' Dr Chettiar said as he walked to his table to write telegrams to be sent to Mr Thevar, Dr Sun Yat-Sen, and Monsieur Verne.

On that first day of his epic journey, Dr Chettiar and Mr Pillai boarded the mail boat to Tuticorin from Egmore railway station. The station had been designed in Gothic style by Henry Irwin and E.C. Bird and when it had opened with its imposing domes, ogival arches, and long corridors, it had been acclaimed as covering a platform area greater than that of Charing Cross Station in London.

Dr Chettiar puffed his Trichinopoly cigar, famed to have been rolled on the thighs of virgin women, whilst he took a sip from his Indian 900 standard silver hip flask.

'Haven't you added more hurdles, Dr Chettiar?' an ageing British member of the press asked as he boarded his train.

'If you love death, life is never a challenge, sir,' he replied and took another puff and added, 'My heart has had the privileged acquaintance with love and death!'

Chapter Two

Day Two

22 June 1907

Madras to Tuticorin

As Mr Pillai sat wondering how he was going to fill the nearly twenty-two hours of the train journey to Tuticorin, Dr Chettiar beckoned him over. Dr Chettiar lit another custom-cut Trichinopoly cigar and said, 'I want you to go to the engine and learn how to operate it.'

The conversation ended there. Dr Chettiar broke off eye contact, having delivered an order which in his head should invoke no further questioning. Dr Chettiar opened *Thirukkural*, the section on *Kama*, which had twenty chapters, and each chapter had ten couplets. He was going to use the time whilst travelling to translate and provide his own interpretation to those 250 couplets. He opened a Moleskin notebook and reached for his Waterman fountain pen with the iridium-tipped gold nib.

He attempted to translate the first couplet:

I believe in death.

An author of the biography of my dreams

The gratified peacock charming monsoon

From the swell of manhood.

The bosoms, mine to elements of greed,

A tremor to my heart.

He could sense *her* presence in every word. Life and love from the past. What had died and what survived? Perhaps he had spent seconds with her translated into syllables and minutes into words. But they lacked form, and that meant he could not write. It was like having energy but no mass; life but no body; memories but no future. He wondered if, in time, thoughts could transform into images of her. His thoughts were interrupted by a loud cry.

'*Koravas*!'

The train was under attack.

Under the Madras Presidency, the *Koravas* had been salt and grain traders. However, when the Criminal Tribes Act of 1871 was passed with the unsavoury intent to demarcate certain tribes as hereditary criminals, *hereditary* being broadly defined, they could be deported, forced into any form of labour, and punished by incarceration. It was not just the perpetrator either but the entire family including any children. With much less choice for livelihoods, these impoverished nomadic tribes were forced into crime.

Dr Chettiar removed his turban and placed it on his seat. He removed his short, single-breasted, unlined, and loose-fitting sack coat, and his patterned necktie. He rolled up the sleeves of his starched blue shirt and ensured that his collar was tidy. He walked out of the compartment and towards the engine and during that stroll, he was deft in knocking off no less than eight of the bandits using *varmam,* a technique that paralysed the arms and legs of these men before tying them with their own dhotis. In this process, he also appeared to have knocked off three or four *company men* who had attempted and on one occasion managed to shoot dead the men who had been unfortunately forced into crime. Thus, largely untested, he opened the carriage door that led to the engine and there in front of him stood a *Korava* who had managed to acquire a double-barrelled howdah pistol from having knocked down the engineer. The *Korava,* in his paranoia, was ready to fire at any moment on Dr Chettiar. A shovel from nowhere hit the *Korava* on the back of the head and as he fell, Dr Chettiar tried holding him to stop him being run over the rails. In that process, Dr Chettiar slipped too and was dangling for his life when Mr Pillai appeared and pulled him up. At that moment, Dr Chettiar re-told the first sonnet he had written, which disappointed Mr Pillai who was expecting to be thanked.

'The bosoms, mine to elements of greed,

A tremor to my heart.'

Dr Chettiar expected to be appreciated but Mr Pillai was in no mood to please his master.

Having saved the *Korava*, Dr Chettiar took a Trichinopoly cigar out from a custom-made case, pulled a beedi from Mr Pillai's mouth and lit his cigar. As he puffed, he formulated a plan.

'Mr Pillai, you have to run the engine until the engineer regains consciousness.'

Dr Chettiar then dragged four *Koravas* to the guard's compartment and treated them for their injuries. He then said to them, 'I am going to release you just before Tuticorin station. I want you to report to Mr Pandithurai Thevar's company at the docks tomorrow morning.'

Tuticorin, one of the ancient seaports of Southern India, had been a settlement for the Portuguese, who had been defeated by the Dutch and, in turn, defeated by the British. It had obtained municipal status in 1866 with Rao Bahadur Cruz Fernandez and JCP Roche Victoria laying foundations for the modern Tuticorin. Tuticorin railway station had been opened in 1874 with the first line connecting Madurai to Tuticorin and in 1899, the Tuticorin-Madras line had been established as part of the Boat Mail to Ceylon.

As the train rolled into the station, none of the passengers seemed to recall the attack. Dr Chettiar was pleased with his mastery of mesmerism.

Mr Pillai and Dr Chettiar were received by Mr Pandithurai Thevar, the zamindar of Palavantham.

'*Vanakkam,*' Dr Chettiar said with his hands folded. Mr Thevar had held Dr Chettiar in high-esteem ever since Dr Chettiar had helped conduct Mrs Thevar's labour. She'd had a complex pregnancy with eclampsia, and the cord had been wrapped around the foetus as well, so Thevar considered Dr Chettiar to be Tiruchendur Murugan himself. The zamindar along with VOC Pillai had just launched the Swadesi Steam Navigation Company and had bought the *SS Galia* from the French.

As they stood admiring *SS Galia*, a manager ran up to them and informed them that 'The captain of the ship has been hospitalised with typhoid!' And with that announcement, Dr Chettiar's plans to sail sank.

Dr Chettiar though did not seem to be troubled and instead said, 'I want to go pearl diving.' Mr Thevar arranged for a dingy helmed by an old and possibly demented Korkai Pandian who had a cataract in his right eye and had lost three fingers on his left hand. He would gladly be rid of his arthritic right hip. Given his limitations, his buxom granddaughter, Poongulali, ran the dinghy. Dr Chettiar would have preferred for her to be the pearl that he would dive for.

A parched thirsty land

I was.

Yet the greedy clouds, your ornate breasts

Could absorb

Any remains sweat, tear and blood

And feed my thirst with

More a nostalgic craving.

Whilst his master was diving for pearl, Mr Pillai struck a conversation with the old man who laughed aloud when he heard about this race around the world.

'Have you heard of the Great Tea Race of 1866?'

Mr Pillai looked blank.

'I was crew on the *Ariel*, fastest of her day. We went across the China Sea, the Indian Ocean, past Mauritius, round the Cape of Africa, to the west of the Azores and led the race as we entered the English Channel. We lost to *Taeping* by twenty-eight minutes as we had to wait at Gravesend. We lost the race but I have the rich experience from it,' Korkai Pandian boasted.

He looked at Poongulali who had heard the story so many times and said, 'If these men hire me, I will captain *SS Galia* to Macao and win the race for them.'

Poongulali remained unimpressed.

Mr Pillai waited patiently for his master to climb aboard the dinghy and for his master to offer the pearl to Poongulali and then dress. He then informed Dr Chettiar about Korkai Pandian.

Dr Chettiar met Mr Thevar on the shore – the latter having returned from offering prayer to Tiruchendur Murugan.

Dr Chettiar said, 'We set sail to Macao at the earliest high tide. Let me introduce you to Captain Pandian!'

Chapter Three

21 June 1907 to 4 July 1907

Day One to Day Fourteen

Madras to Hong Kong

Lord Edward Harris was a tall man with chiselled features, pointed-nose, and luxurious sideburns that ran all the way down to his jaw. The Honourable Harris was born in Bombay where his father was then serving as governor. When he was two, his mother died, subsequent to which, the family moved to Madras, and when his father retired, they returned to England to settle in rural Kent. Lord Harris, apart from being prodigious in tennis and cricket, fell in love with Byron and Tchaikovsky, especially when he heard the Manfred Symphony.

An Etonian, he obtained commission at the Royal Military Academy, Sandhurst and served in the infantry wearing a red coat and a Sam Browne belt. He showed his marksmanship with the Webley revolver, and he distinguished himself by being mentioned in Lord Kitchener's despatches from the Battle of Ombduran in 1898. It would be the last time he had to wear the red coat before being promoted to lieutenant-colonel, dressed in khaki, decorated with the insignia of a star beneath the crown, and posted to Madras.

On the journey from Brindisi, Lord Harris took a week off in Ceylon, where he saw her for the first time.

Time would thus be captured;

How be it, nor thy lips, nor thy face,

Why even thine eyes, the twin Suns,

And bosoms, moons that wax not wane

To thy Southern planet where life thrives;

But the air around thee countenance smiles

A contagion to creation invisible to eyes;

Adding breath fragrant with inferno

Vigorous to not melt or freeze dew drops

Virginal, that moment between defeat and victory

Thy arrested it between thy little toe and next

In shyness, they wince, and further suffocate Time.

Time, invincible, timeless, a second it missed,

That moment in love thy fell, love I wasn't kissed.

It must be noted that centuries on the cricket pitch had since that moment faded in comparison to his challenge to write at least one more sonnet than Shakespeare, whom he respected only next to Lord Byron.

He had just got off a jinrikisha outside the Grand Hotel and was looking forward to his evening meal of duck curry when he saw the spectacle of a lady getting into a hydrogen balloon, The Canary. She was attempting to perform the first night ride by a female balloonist. Her eyes met his heart. A heart that failed to beat for the next fourteen-and-a-half hours as she was trapped in a hail storm and eventually landed the following morning with a nose bleed, icicles, and having lost consciousness for at least a third of the time she was inflight.

As he waited on the veranda of the Grand Hotel, she walked out on her way to the Pharsee Theatre. Her bird-like features made him believe that his life would be the sky for her to soar. He went up to her and before he could open his mouth she said, 'Lord Harris! How do you do?'

She surprised him. 'Miss Joanna Roberts.' He bowed and kissed her hand.

Miss Roberts was beautiful and perhaps made more beautiful by a tinge of sadness that had found an outlet in her attraction towards adventures that put her life at risk. Defeating death would be the best expression if not evidence for life; the gentle golden-brown hue to her otherwise pink skin would bear testament to coming out of such pyrrhic experiences in life. There was a lock of shining hair that swept across her forehead, which sometimes she played with and made into knots and then blowing on it. She ensured that the strength of her heart was what people saw as even her dimples never came out at in public.

'I wonder if you would kindly join me for tea?' he requested.

'I am afraid I am on my way to the theatre. Perhaps if you are happy to wait until I return later in the evening for dinner?'

When she returned that evening, their eyes met and she smiled.

'Good evening, Lord Harris. Would you mind if Dr Vellingiri Chettiar, my friend from my time in Cambridge, joined us too?'

As they laughed and dined – well, Dr Chettiar and Miss Roberts did – Lord Harris had his nemesis nudge him and whisper, 'Don't have your hopes high, my friend. Neither men, nor their sports – and least of all cricket – impress Joanna.'

And later when they walked to the smoking-room he said, 'I feel for you, Lord Harris, I really do. If you are after conquering her heart, do something audacious. You know, go to the Poles, climb a mountain, or go *around the world…*'

It did not have to be said that the second sonnet he penned later that night was very different and ended thus:

'I sit by thy side and watch thee in love, eyes closed, heart open

With my meagre love nothing more than to fill my pen.'

He would meet with her again when he'd find excuses to visit Governor Roberts, her father, and he learnt that she had been homeschooled and then had become interested in science to achieve her ambition of flying. She would recall her days in Cambridge with HRH Karishma Kaur, her then friend, and Dr Chettiar with such fondness; how he had not managed to break the China he held every time Dr Chettiar's name came up remains to be discovered by science. He was also introduced by her to HRH Senbaga Valli Nachiyar, who always accompanied Miss Roberts every time he invited her to watch him play cricket. He was struggling to keep HRH Nachiyar and Miss Roberts separate and there was tension in the air. And that tension was not just due to a frustrated Lord Harris.

He read another sonnet for her:

'I write this jocund as a ripple in that pond

Made by the pebble you threw, thy love, thy bow.'

There was one problem though, Miss Roberts despised poetry. HRH Nachiyar though admired his writings.

Lord Harris believed with the strength of his love that, Miss Roberts must have endured a tragedy in her childhood that had taken away from her the succour and sustenance that poetry could provide. Although he wished to be the only person she could confide that rancour in her heart, he had to be content when she said to him, 'After much persuasion, Dr Chettiar has agreed to be my therapist!'

When she said that, his initial reaction was to believe that he had to go far away from all of this, far away from her, except that the farthest he could go even mentally had to be the quickest he returned to her. That along with Dr Chettiar's words in Ceylon, sowed seeds for that journey, to go farther but to come back quicker, quicker than anyone else had ever done; to go around the world fastest, and then to kneel down in front of her. Yes, that would, and not poetic stanzas or cricketing stances would make her see his love for her. Why, it would even make her accept his love for her.

Early that fateful day when Governor Roberts was murdered at the Madras Cricket Club, Lord Harris had been with Governor Roberts at the latter's office at Fort St George. Governor Roberts seemed to be preoccupied following a visit from Mr One Too-Many and was dealing with papers related to an Arab pirate Barut who was awaiting sentencing with the ship *Al Kahila* ready to be impounded at any moment.

Miss Roberts and HRH Nachiyar stormed into Governor Roberts' office, hauling behind them an evil man who supplied to the elite of Madras any form of life to meet their needs of sexual perversion. It had taken the ladies about three days from the time HRH Nachiyar had sought assistance from her friend Miss Roberts. The latter was involved in taking care of the welfare of the children of Black Town and helped with finding boys and girls disappearing from Ramanathapuram whilst the officers chased the papers more than the people involved.

'He needs to be shot dead, Papa,' she vented in fury, and no sooner than she had requested it then Governor Roberts took Lord Harris's Colt single action army revolver that he'd been admiring moments previously and shot the man dead.

'Papa!' Miss Roberts shrieked in horror and fainted whilst Lord Harris ensured that he was there to catch her. Governor Roberts was hailed of God of Instant Justice by the people and the press.

The last he'd seen of her was at the Madras Cricket Club when she'd arrived with her father for the ball before the entire world changed with the murder of Governor Roberts. And then he had heard her shriek.

Hence that night when he boarded the *Carnatic* and set sail for Hong Kong on the first leg of his race around the world, he was shocked when he opened his trunk.

There was Miss Roberts, unconscious inside.

He made her sit up and offered her whisky but throughout the journey she barely ate or drank and, even more worryingly, she just repeated one thing in response to several questions he had asked.

'What happened?'

'What did you see?'

'Who killed your papa?'

The answer was always the same.

So, when the *Carnatic* docked at Hong Kong and Inspector Davies greeted them at the port and informed them that neither Lord Harris nor Miss Roberts could travel further until the murderer of Governor Roberts could be brought to justice, he knew what he had to arrange to ensure that his journey around the world would not be compromised and be content that the journey of his nemesis would be jeopardised.

He said, 'Inspector Davies, you should hear what Miss Roberts has to say as a witness who was present when her father was murdered.'

When Inspector Davies arrived to interrogate Miss Roberts, Lord Harris ensured that he would not ask Miss Roberts all the questions he had asked previously but just one question, for the inspector did not have to know just then that the answer to all questions would be one and the same.

'Miss Roberts, can you please tell this inspector who shot your father, Governor Roberts?'

She looked as if the darkness that had consumed all her life was now replaced with light that but blinded her and replied, 'Dr Vellingiri Chettiar.'

Chapter Four

22 June 1907

Day Two

Madras

Mr One Too-Many was in his fifties. He had been born in London. And he had the smallest heart ever known to mankind. And as every person with a small heart had ever done, he too desired to possess everything in this world. As the owner of the smallest of hearts, he believed firmly that only he should be allowed to possess everything in this world. It needs to be mentioned that the reason for the reduction in the size of his heart was the hurt inflicted upon him ever since he had been born, by the beasts in this world. Why, even when he was conceived by a man who had disappeared after purging his semen, and a woman, who herself had lost her childhood that day she realised she had fallen pregnant. No one could recall the origins of his surname or Christian name, for he need not have been a Christian even. He'd had to break every rule of life and law of the land to learn about living. And then he'd had to learn to break those without being caught and to master the art of survival. One of his male masters who preferred boys, taught him English and he learnt arithmetic from managing books with money he collected in trade and lost in trauma.

When he grew up and was no more a boy, he was no longer needed in London. He resorted to crime but he got caught twice and sentenced to, on the first occasion for stealing bread, fourteen days of gaol in Bedford and to be whipped; on the second occasion, he was sentenced to hard labour for six months for stealing bread, meat, and cheese. On release, as every self-respecting man of his times did, he found passage on a ship bound for the colonies, and his destination was Hindustan.

There was not much left of his body that had failed to develop from malnutrition, and what had developed had withered away in syphilis and hence he wasn't tested by the vagaries of the sea. And given that his language would truly not have absorbed Milton and Keats, the vacuum in his brain was readily filled with native tongues and customs. Though he had knowledge and skills in breaking the law, such deftness was rarely needed in a colony, for he lived in times that colour of skin gave right to most if not all wrongs and if not his genealogy then his anaemia gave him the required amount of paleness. And so parched was he that, he could take on any colour that his superior officers wanted him to apply to himself, first in the Presidency of Bombay and then in the Presidency of Madras.

There was one moment in his life when he could have changed course and for that brief length of time, he had been in love with a memsahib. He had even obtained her promise to marry, but love just wasn't enough for life. When an offer knocked on his door, to move up ranks, and it involved Rangoon, he opted for it and without regrets; the offer had been made to him by this memsahib's father himself. One could argue about who was playing Devil and who was playing God, but that not only would that be a waste of time but the answer would also change and too many times at that.

He found on his return to Madras that being a secretary to anyone with power provided him with the spoils at least and an illusion of riches; and when his superior officers found that he put loyalty ahead of morality, he became indispensable to the gentlemen and officers. It had been a perfect run until he had been appointed as chief of staff to Dr Chettiar. As much as Dr Chettiar was a connoisseur for pleasure, he refrained from corrupt measures to provide pleasure to his mind. Hence for a brief period, Mr Too-Many had to manage his income and indulgence within the penal codes, civil and criminal.

It would have remained thus, had Governor Roberts not had a protracted admission for anal fistula and Mr Too-Many ended up reviewing him more than the doctors ever did. He came to know that Governor Roberts believed that he was Lord Krishna and was always scouting for *gopikas.*

Margazhi full moon.

Brimming with wisdom, this auspicious day

Witness fine blossoming girls in Ayarpadi with bounteous bosoms

Perfect and

This Nandagopan, youth, sadistic, his work with a sharp spear

This young cub of Yashoda with passionate eyes

Has lustrous visage dark as black clouds

Definitive red eyes

Face radiant as the rays of the moon borrowed from the sun.

Narayanan, shall deliver us with drums.

Join us, the people of worlds in celebration!

It was this, Aandal's *Thirupaavai,* that Governor Roberts prescribed to. And Mr One Too-Many became a procurer of *gopikas.* Of course, occasional *gopi* too. His henchman was one Kalingarayan. And for exotic needs, he had struck a business deal with Barut, who led a pirate gang on the Arabian Seas.

It was all going fine until HRH Senbaga Valli Nachiyar of Ramanathapuram, the titular princess, intruded.

HRH Nachiyar had taken to formal education and had completed the PUC. She could speak Tamil, Urdu, French and English. She was trained in *ottam tullal* and had been praised for her *tanam.* She practised *silambam vallavi* and *varmam.* Her husband from a child marriage had died when she was twelve and that too on the night after marriage. Although the Kingdom of Ramanathapuram was under the British, she remained the people's princess. When she heard about a series of boys and girls disappearing under inexplicable circumstances, she decided to investigate herself. Her courtiers and British officers had refined the art of the leisurely travel of papers from one desk to another. With the progression of civilisation thus curtailed by such officers, rank and file, she sought help from her best friend in Madras, Miss Joanna Roberts.

Between the two ladies, it took seventy-two hours. Those who confessed were sent to jail; those who refused were left to rot six feet under. And in those seventy-two hours, they tracked down a major player in Madras, the man who was eventually shot dead by Governor Roberts, the latter who then became hailed as the God of Justice.

Mr One Too-Many had been at the infamous Madras Cricket Club on the day Governor Roberts had been murdered; and he had witnessed that boy, whom he had left with Governor Roberts, being hurriedly removed from there by a native. He had seen Dr Chettiar rush to get hold of the Colt Single Action Army revolver, and he also saw a stranger carrying away Miss Roberts who was unconscious, and there was Lord Harris too at the scene. He chose to follow the stranger who was carrying Miss Roberts and who deposited her into a trunk inside a carriage stationed outside the cupola. He attempted to follow the stranger further except that when the stranger turned and touched his forehead, he went into a deep slumber.

When he woke up, he had questions. He had more questions when he saw the Colt Single Action Army revolver proudly displayed along with Dr Chettiar's toothbrush. He experienced something he hadn't since he had been a boy on the streets of London. Fear. He was frightened that people in the know might come after him. He would have to deal with such people and amongst them could be Dr Chettiar, Miss Roberts, Lord Harris, and that stranger.

So, he went to Kalingarayan. He had to strike first.

After that, he went to the police commissioner with evidence that pointed to the murderer of Governor Roberts. If Kalingarayan failed, the law would take its own course and, for once, assist Mr One Too-Many.

Chapter Five

Some day in July 1907

About Day Twenty

Tuticorin to Macao

Dr Chettiar's world had turned upside down – in a metaphorical and literal sense. He had been hung upside down from the topmast of the *SS Galia.* As had Mr Pillai who was hanging from the other end of the rope, with both parties maintaining a precarious balance. The screw steamer with an iconic hull, four-horse-power engine and weighing 1770 tonnes, having passed the Strait of Malacca and sailing on to the South China Sea, had a new captain. Its destination was now not Macao but the Queen Victoria port in Hong Kong, a British territory.

The SS Galia set sail from Tuticorin under the stewardship of Captain Pandian, assisted by Poongulali with instructions from Dr Chettiar. They would have to arrive in Macao in less than a fortnight. That would negate at least the day's advantage that Lord Harris held over Dr Chettiar. Mr Pillai had stocked the ship with provisions. Some of the crew had served under the previous captain of the SS Galia and another four were employed from the band of *Koravas* that had been pardoned by Dr Chettiar much against the wishes of the Thevar who had conceded to Dr Chettiar's argument that these men did need a fair opportunity in life. They worked as hard as the seasoned crew, as every member of staff had been promised twice their pay should they arrive in Macao in under fourteen days.

It took twenty-four hours and abundant opium for Captain Pandian to establish his mastery over the ship and earn the respect of his crew. By the time they passed the Andaman Saddle Peak at a height of 2400 ft, Poongulali had impressed the seafarers with her deftness for efficient management of the compound steam engine that used exhaust steam from high-pressure cylinders to low-pressure cylinders. And with such hope, everyone onboard believed that they could defeat time.

Dr Chettiar was hanging from his bed upside down with his head touching the wooden floor of his cabin. A phial of opium was within knocking distance from his head. His finger was using ash from the stub of a cigar stub to write his thoughts on the floor as he spoke.

'I have

Wrestled with the dark fiery magma

From your bounteous bosoms.

Stood brave as the erected column of pleasure

To the torrents of your melodious heaving breath

Fluted your uberous earth

With my coffin.

My inebriated tongue

Has been the rock that withstood

The tsunami waves from the crests of your lips

And my nails demolished the uneventful sky,

Your back, with more crescents and stars,

But your furnace of passion in thine eyes

Whipped with chants and spells from the witches on your eyelashes

Defeat me and my language

Into episodes of rapacious cries

Linked by mercenary silence.'

He was wearing nothing but the thin silver *manimekalai* that belonged to Poongulali. And even that was adorning the wrong place; it had been tied around his hands.

'Mr Pillai!' he shouted. He needed to be released yet again.

Mr Pillai had been entrusted with the affairs of the men and one woman aboard the SS Galia. He was also burdened with maintaining a journal of the voyage. And he could deal with everything and everyone but for his master who never subscribed to the concept of time. He had been awoken anytime between midnight and dawn – to practice fencing; then it would be for experimenting on alcohol and opium; for making a meal because his master had forgotten to eat during the day. If there had been some expectation of respite during the day, that was quashed with much disdain. Dr Chettiar would ask him to sit and listen to his translation. And when he was stuck, he would stare at Mr Pillai.

On one such occasion –

'Even water

The drug of universal dependence

Should be drunk for survival

But for your nubile beauty

Tangible not to touch…' Dr Chettiar was lost for words and ordered Mr Pillai not to move from his chair, whilst Dr Chettiar himself persisted in his favourite posture – hanging from his bed upside down. And it was no less than an hour and forty minutes before Dr Chettiar could come up with the final verses:

'But hydros to my stoma

With chlorophyll

Turning photons into…'

And whilst Mr Pillai braced himself for another hour at least, he finished, 'Opium!' and grabbed his liquid pleasure.

If that was tolerable, then Mr Pillai also operated a messenger service; for Poongulali – who had dreamt of the proverbial journey across the seven seas and seven continents in search of a prince who'd been excommunicated from his kingdom following the treacherous murder of the king by his brother – Dr Chettiar was but the perfect match. She was the dynamite for his spark. He was the pain for her pleasure. At the end of their congress, the term preferred by Dr Chettiar, she would leave him tied up in unimaginable postures and it had become one of Mr Pillai's chores to rescue his master.

There were times when he even wondered if Dr Chettiar was focused on the race and more recently had been keen to know the progress made by Lord Harris. He could not imagine, or at least certainly hoped that Lord Harris would not be lost on such sensual pleasures, and reassured himself that Lord Harris would be meticulous and cautious. He trusted his belief and this was important to him.

Unlike, of course, Dr Chettiar. For when he shouted for Mr Pillai on that day, not Mr Pillai but a *Korava* who had a dagger held between his turban and his ear, entered holding an Enfield rifle pointed at Dr Chettiar.

'Kalingarayan!' Dr Chettiar smiled. This was not reciprocated because the butt of the revolver knocked him unconscious and when he woke up, as described earlier, he was hanging from the mast upside down.

Kalingarayan was but the digestive system for Mr One Too-Many. To be more specific, his bowels. He would process orders from Mr One Too-Many and either turn them into nutrients or excrete them. And this time, he had been tasked with the job of killing Dr Chettiar. When his first attempt at killing Dr Chettiar whilst on the train had failed, he had received instructions that Dr Chettiar's voyage to Macao had to be delayed and, if possible, the ship needed to be rerouted to the British territory of Hong Kong. There, Kalingarayan would be suitably recognised and rewarded for capturing the man who had murdered Governor Roberts.

Dr Chettiar unwittingly had been only too willing to facilitate this treacherous plan when he'd invited the Koravas to work on the ship. And it need not be said that the original captain of the SS Galia would have been found on autopsy to have died from poisoning and not typhoid, yet this would never be attributed to Kalingarayan.

It was time for Kalingarayan to commandeer the SS Galia. This, in fact, had required very little bloodshed. Once two of the regular seamen were cut to death with the only aim of creating fear amongst the other crew, Kalingarayan had the control of the ship. Poongulali had been taken hostage. Pandian, not captain anymore, had his arm tied to the wheel. He was left with no choice but to steer to Hong Kong as his granddaughter's life was at stake.

Kalingarayan returned to Dr Chettiar and Mr Pillai. He had ensured that Dr Chettiar was blindfolded so that *noku varmam* would be negated. Unfortunately for him though, a storm arrived. And with it the sea erupted, each wave wanting to suck the ship to its abyss. The wind, if it did not blow any of them to a distant universe, cut through the exposed and dug out the unexposed parts of anyone or anything; living or dead.

The Korava who had been standing guard by Pandian and Poongulali was knocked by a gust of wind and his sword fell within the reach of Pandian. Poongulali looked at her grandfather and her eyes said, 'Do something, old man! Be heroic for once in your life!'

The storm swung the rope from which Dr Chettiar and Mr Pillai were hanging and before they could realise it, the rope had fallen to the railing with Dr Chettiar on the deck and Mr Pillai lashed by the waves. The latter was being asphyxiated.

There appeared on the deck an old diminutive man with a gigantic shadow. When lightning struck, he appeared with one arm holding a sword. He had just one arm. His other arm was still chained to the wheel. The sword was dripping with blood. He fainted but not before he threw that sword to Dr Chettiar.

A duel ensued between Dr Chettiar with his hands still tied together, eyes blindfolded and his movement controlled to ensure that Mr Pillai's head was not submerged in the sea. Kalingarayan slashed across Dr Chettiar's chest. But that was a ruse. The doctor who was an expert in anatomy wanted his attacker just where he could stab between Kalingarayan's ribs with surgical precision. This battle of death even frightened the storm that had until then savaged the ship and its occupants. Once Kalingarayan fell, Dr Chettiar released himself and pulled Mr Pillai out. He started thumping Mr Pillai's chest but with a strange frown followed by an even stranger smile on his face. As inappropriate it would seem, his lips voiced another couplet that he had thus far struggled to translate:

'This small space

On top of your bud

A mine for all pleasures of the future.

In this moment

In the crimson dusk of life

Now you are, then gone…'

When Mr Pillai came back to life, Dr Chettiar went to look at Kalingarayan who said, 'Too-Many,' before he stopped breathing. Poongulali appeared on the deck, holding a revolver in one arm and a sword in another. Her wet clothes revealed her throbbing breasts and she looked like Goddess Kali herself. She had killed two other Koravas and the original crew had now taken to their usual positions.

'Mr Pillai, we need to save Captain Pandian,' Dr Chettiar said as he knelt by the veteran seafarer.

The dining hall became an operating theatre for Dr Chettiar to stem the haemorrhage and stop Captain Pandian from dying. After fourteen hours, the veteran regained consciousness. And this time when Poongulali embraced Dr Chettiar, he was for once, not left tied up in any unimaginable posture.

When the eyes of our senses meet

They create a tremble

The flicker of wings of a butterfly

That opens your floral lips

Into rhythms and waves of delicate smiles.

Unseen, but palpable.

Delayed for thirty-six hours, they sailed into Macao.

Chapter Six

4 July 1907

Day Fourteen

Arrival in Hong Kong

Hong Kong was a terraced city with radiant white mansions on the tall mountainside. The picturesque bay surrounded by mountains reminded Lord Harris of cupping Miss Roberts' luminescent face by the cheeks. And just as Miss Roberts' face would be dotted with expressions of doubt, the bay was populated densely with iron-clads, torpedo boats, *lorchas*, and Chinese ships with enormous sterns and magnificent bows. With *The Oceanic* due to sail for Yokohama the following evening, Lord Harris and Miss Roberts were carried on sedans by pig-tailed Chinese men beyond warehouses, balconied buildings populated with Chinese families, a skyline coloured with myriad clotheslines, and streets crowded by mankind with dishevelled clothes and derailed hopes, fed upon and fed with opium until they reached Hotel Craigieburn.

Whilst Miss Roberts convalesced, Lord Harris dined with the proprietor who suggested a visit to Victoria Peak, which, at 1800 feet high, was the highest point on the island. Lord Harris dismissed the suggestion as it neither offered solace to his heart or a solution to his head.

As Lord Harris poured oolong tea, Inspector Davies arrived. Inspector Davies was a logarithmic table. Everything was precise and predictable. Linear. For such a man, there was no necessity for flesh but only as required in minimal quantity to maintain his athleticism even as he had just turned sixty the previous week. He did not perhaps see a need for hair, hence his bald head shone in the red light, and perhaps it was his neurons that lit up and created that halo. His sartorial preference had not changed with the times or weather or land or customs. A burgundy red frock coat that had but vestiges of that colour and had come to fade with the vagaries of time; a black necktie that had more stains than in the hearts of the criminals he had arrested over the years; a vest that even a spider would forfeit; and fly-front trousers, the colour of which, like God, was perceived by the believers and beholders based on their faith. This lean and tall man with eyes that could cut through diamond sat opposite Lord Harris.

'Lord Harris, I have a couple of things to talk about,' he said.

Lord Harris appeared earnest. His heart that had withheld truth now sought confirmation of the truth that the world thus far believed.

'I have been informed that the gun that was used to murder Governor Roberts has been found.'

Inspector Davies paused. He believed that silence made truth reveal itself through facial expressions. And Lord Harris, after years and battles under Lord Kitchener was versed in the art of holding his breath to survive, as contradictory as that might seem.

'Mr One Too-Many reported the gun to the police commissioner at Madras. It was found in the bathroom of Dr Chettiar's residence.'

Whilst Lord Harris's heart fibrillated in happiness, his eyes fluttered in shock. Was it true that Miss Roberts had indeed witnessed her father's murder by Dr Chettiar?

'A warrant has been issued for Dr Chettiar's arrest,' Inspector Davies informed Lord Harris.

'Thank you for informing me,' Lord Harris said and the inspector stood to leave.

'Inspector Davies,' Lord Harris said as they started walking to the foyer. 'I believe Dr Chettiar, if lucky, will be taking a route that will make him sail to Macao and then to Yokohama, followed by San Francisco.'

'I look forward to arresting him in San Francisco,' Inspector Davies confirmed.

'In that case, I would be pleased if you would prefer to travel with Miss Roberts and myself as we travel to Yokohama and then to San Francisco,' Lord Harris invited him, and continued, '*The Oceanic* of the Oriental and Occidental Steamship Company sets sail tomorrow evening.'

'Lord Harris, your gesture would be much appreciated by His Majesty's government.'

Later that evening, a relieved Lord Harris arranged for jinrikishas to carry Miss Roberts and himself through the Happy Valley where every February, races were held with native bred Mongolian ponies. The sight of the graveyards of the Fire-Worshippers, Presbyterians, Episcopalians, Methodists, Catholics and Mohammadens close by each other reinforced his belief that such equality even after death would only happen in the British Empire. Absorbed in his thoughts, he failed to observe the fire in Miss Roberts' eyes.

They reached a theatre where the Amateur Dramatics Club of Hong Kong, which comprised of eager and enthusiastic men from the regiments, performed Aladdin and the Magic Lamp, with music conducted by the bandmaster of the Argyll and Sutherland Highlanders.

'Why could the third wish not always be for three more wishes?' Lord Harris wondered. Lost in his thoughts, he did not observe the rage in Miss Roberts' face as the young Aladdin was left to die by his sadistic uncle.

The Oceanic launched by Mr Hartland of Belfast was the first to introduce saloon amidships, and this greyhound of the Atlantic was transferred to the Pacific, retaining its luxurious ambience, and exquisite catering. The Social Hall was filled with nostalgic tales and passionate dreams. The captain played the organette and when Inspector Davies realised that apart from reliving ball-by-ball England's 2-0 victory under Stanley Jackson over Australia, the only other contribution he could make was to show his skills on the organette.

'Archie Maclaren and his swashbuckling 140,' Lord Harris said was the reason for the English victory in the first test. He had been awestruck of his contemporary ever since the fast and stylish right-handed batsman had scored 424 for Lancashire against Somerset.

'Bernard Bosanquet, eight for 107,' Inspector Davies argued. There was more merit in his argument for this Middlesex cricketer had been recognised by The Wisden as cricketer of the year in 1905.

On the last night before they were due to arrive in Yokohama, dinner was accompanied by punch and champagne and oysters. Over dinner, Lord Harris mentioned his thoughts about Aladdin and the Magic Lamp, including his perspective about the three wishes. Inspector Davies did not fail to notice Miss Roberts' eyes spit fire when they talked about the plight of young Aladdin at the merciless hands of his wretched uncle.

Hence, that night when Inspector Davies returned to his cabin that was next to the suite occupied by Lord Harris, which had a private chamber for Miss Roberts, even the Caribbean melodies sung by the men in the smoking-room beneath his cabin could not lull him to sleep. So it was no surprise that when the melody was interrupted by a gunshot, he was the first to arrive at the scene, breaking through the door to enter Lord Harris's suite, where he witnessed Miss Roberts having failed in her first attempt, point the gun again at Lord Harris. He flung himself at her but she had fired a bullet.

CHAPTER SEVEN

21 July 1907

Day Thirty-One

Arrival in Macao

Macao. Dr Chettiar was sat in the library at Dr Sun Yat-Sen's house, dressed in an impeccable morning coat, narrow trousers and bow tie in green. He looked bemusedly at Captain Pandian who was pointing a 0.476 calibre Mark II Enfield revolver at Dr Chettiar.

'Be careful with that complex machine, Captain Pandian. I am not a fan of the Owen Jones complicated system,' he said, unperturbed that the very man he had saved from near-death was now ready to kill him.

'The congress was in a lion's den.

In that moment

When the eyes of pleasure became unanimous

The beasts of the den

Swore allegiance to ahimsa,' he recited his composition.

'I do believe in ahimsa,' Dr Chettiar reiterated.

Captain Pandian was unmoved. His life's purpose seemed bent on unleashing 18gr of black powder and a 265-gram lead bullet from the revolver.

'Dr Chettiar, I would have to kill you if you don't–'

Dr Sun Yat-Sen had been one of the recipients of the telegrams that Dr Chettiar had arranged to be sent before leaving on this grandiose expedition around the world, and he looked forward to the acquaintance of the man whom he had first met at the Hong Kong College of Medicine. Dr Chettiar had then been a visiting student. Their love for medicine was only rivalled by their love for adventure and Dr Chettiar had been one of the first doctors to congratulate Dr Sun Yat-Sen when the latter was invited to set up the Western medicine department at the Kiang Wu Hospital in Macao. Dr Chettiar had then invested in his peer's Chinese-Western medicine joint clinic in Rue das Estalagens. He had promised to visit Dr Sun Yat-Sen and give a lecture and this voyage had provided him with just that opportunity.

Macao was Portuguese. The Sino-Portuguese Treaty of Peking left ample scope for interpretation by both parties. Its heydays as the entry point for opium into China was terminated by the First Opium War and by the establishment of Hong Kong. Presently, its faltering economy depended on tea and tobacco processing and firecracker and incense production.

Dr Chettiar, Mr Pillai, Captain Pandian and Poongulali were lodged at Dr Sun Yat-Sen's residence. Lunch that day included pig's ear and papaya salad, and rabbit served in wine, cinnamon, and star anise. Mr Pillai and Captain Pandian refrained from eating pork. Poongulali had Dr Chettiar for entrée and followed that with pork and stew.

Dr Chettiar enthralled his friend by reading excerpts from his translation:

'A poison in the pitcher of yours

And a cure in the chalice.'

Later that afternoon, Dr Sun Yat-Sen took Dr Chettiar to the port. Dr Sun Yat-Sen impressed upon Dr Chettiar with his ideology, '*Minzu, Minguan, and Minsheng.* I am not sure if my skills in translation are as good as yours, Dr Chettiar, but it means nationalism, the rights of people, and scientific study to help people survive in society,' he said in English.

Before them stood *A-Ma*, named after the God to whom the first structure in Macao was built in 1368. *A-Ma,* at twenty tonnes, was a fast-sailing yacht. She had two masts, was well-rigged, and had proven her mettle by winning several prizes in the pilot-boat races. *A-Ma's* crew was led by Captain Burbage, whose heart was on fire with rum and whose head was an encyclopaedia of experiences.

'I have failed several times, Dr Chettiar,' he had declared with pride. 'And hence I know what success means.'

Below the deck were two suites that were furnished sparsely yet efficiently. *A-Ma* sailed under a Portuguese flag.

'I understand that we are to set sail to Yokohama tomorrow,' Mr Burbage said.

'At three in the afternoon, I have been informed by Dr Sun Yat-Sen,' Dr Chettiar confirmed.

'I am told that your aim though is to reach San Francisco,' a pensive Captain Burbage remarked. He then put his hat back on and said, 'Godspeed, Dr Chettiar!'

Later that evening, when he stood next to a blackboard that had 'Alzheimer's disease' written on it with white chalk, Dr Chettiar said, 'Let us give credit where it is due,' and struck off Alzheimer's disease and instead scribbled 'Fisher's disease.' He delivered his lecture.

The following morning, Mr Pillai could feel the tension in the air. Poongulali was supervising the stock needed for the *SS Galia* to make its return journey to Tuticorin. Dr Sun Yat-Sen had arranged for a Portuguese mariner to captain the ship back to Tuticorin. Captain Pandian was nowhere to be seen. Mr Pillai had assumed that Captain Pandian was either suffering from a hangover or was unhappy at having his captaincy revoked.

He was proven wrong when he walked into the library with Poongulali to find Captain Pandian finishing his sentence with the words '...marry Poongulali.'

Dr Chettiar did not even pretend to consider this option. 'No, Captain Pandian.'

'*Thatha!*' Poongulali shouted in anger and walked between the Enfield and Dr Chettiar. She held the gun and said in a measured tone, 'I would not want to marry this man.'

The grandfather burst into tears as he asked, 'But what will the world say about you?'

She removed the revolver from his hand and replied, 'It can't say any worse than what would be said if I married and lived with a man who didn't know love.'

She then turned to Dr Chettiar and recited a poem she had penned:

'As we part, and you walk beyond the paddy field

My armpits smell

Not of the mirth from your hard manhood

But from the gore, from my soft heart.'

As they walked away, she handed the revolver to Mr Pillai who felt that the damage the bullet could never have done, Poongulali's words had.

Dr Chettiar looked defeated. His mind was lost to the past. Mr Pillai wondered what that head could hold. Dr Chettiar took his pen and wrote:

'I spend my loneliness by the molten river

Inhaling volcanic ash.

The absence of your breasts to touch is my murder.

The absence of your breasts to feel is my suicide.'

That afternoon, Dr Chettiar bid farewell to Dr Sun Yat-Sen and boarded *A-Ma* with Mr Pillai.

'Are we ready to sail, Captain Burbage?' he asked.

The captain replied, 'Yes, Dr Chettiar, to San Francisco!'

CHAPTER EIGHT

13 July 1907

Day Twenty-Three

Arrival in Yokohama

Yokohama was a port city on the island of Honshu with access to Tokyo Bay. Yokohama meant horizontal beach. The city had humble origins as a fishing village from a sandbar that appeared horizontal when viewed from the sea. Further to the Treaty of Peace and Amity with the USA, Yokohama had become one of the Japanese ports open to foreign ships. Yokohama port was officially opened on the 2 June 1859. The Yamate district, known by the English-speaking residents as the Bluff, became the residential area for the foreigners. The British military garrison was established in 1862 to further British commercial and diplomatic interests. Cricket had been played there since 1863. After the Maji restoration of 1868, Yokohama port became the centre for silk trade with Britain. Samuel Corking built the city's first power plant in 1887, which in time became the Yokohama Co-operative Electric Light Company.

Inspector Davies sat reading the Japanese Herald, which had been published since 1861. He was admiring a reprint of the Samurai of the Satsuma Clan during the British War period (1868–1869) photographed by ace Venetian photographer Felice Beato.

On a bed nearby, Lord Harris opened his eyes. He heard his sonnet but in Dr Chettiar's voice.

On waking, how do thy first feel thy love?

Would it be like the first rays of the sun

That awaken a farmer? But it takes six seconds for rays to reach the Earth.

Would it be like the first kick felt by a pregnant mother? But their blood would have embraced since conception.

Would it be like a truth about life found in old age? but it would have always been there to be discovered.

Would it be like the words first spoken by a child? But the sounds make more meaning than abstract words.

Would it be like the first creation of art, a painting or a poem? But it was just a copy of nature that showed everything to those who sensed with their minds.

Does thy feel love like being born again? Becoming an Earth again?

My love, it's felt first each dawn as death. Always in pain.

'Have we missed the ship?' he sounded as if the answer to that question would help him decide whether he should live or die.

'The *SS Grant* leaves this evening, Lord Harris,' Inspector Davies replied. Inspector Davies was brief. He was used to letting his action speak volumes and his words, perhaps, used as punctuation marks at most.

By the time he'd lunged at Miss Roberts, she had already fired. The bullet had gone through Lord Harris's thigh, narrowly missing the femur and femoral artery. The surgeon at Juzen Hospital in Yokohama had removed the bullet and bandaged the flesh wound.

Inspector Davies had, since leaving Lord Harris under the care of the surgeon, visited the British military garrison. He had sent a telegram to Madras, and the reply that he hoped to receive before they left Yokohama would help him proceed with his investigation into the murder of Governor Roberts.

He also had a responsibility towards Miss Roberts. The captain of *The Oceanic* helped him administer laudanum to her. She was now resting in her cabin on the *SS Grant* under the supervision of the staff he had employed at His Majesty's expenditure. As he was sipping beer, produced in Japan since 1865, he replayed the last night onboard The Oceanic. Miss Roberts had been unhappy, why, even angry. Aladdin. Boy. Uncle. Lord Harris shot at twice by Miss Roberts. She was now under arrest for the attempted murder of Lord Harris. Why would she attempt killing Lord Harris when he was her guardian? He thought about the murder of Governor Roberts. Miss Roberts had said the name of Dr Chettiar in response to his questioning. And the gun had been found in Dr Chettiar's house. His fingerprints were on it. But what would Dr Chettiar's motive have been? Why would a man who had just challenged Lord Harris to a race around the world, then decide to go and murder Governor Roberts?

Was this race a distraction? And then there was Miss Roberts and her strange behaviour. Was it Kraepelin's psychosis? Or Freud's penis envy? And Lord Harris, this grudge he held for Dr Chettiar; was that a driver for the accusations he made? Yet, what had he done to be shot?

He hoped that the telegram from Madras would answer his questions. As he walked back from the bar, the contradictions of Yokohama struck him – on one side was the affluent Bluff area with foreign settlers and the other side Kojiki-Yato, the largest slum in Japan with Japanese and Korean vagrants. Every modern city was starting to face this problem.

Lord Harris had fallen in love with the Japanese language and the country's traditions when he had been crew to the fifth Marquess of Lansdowne, who'd brought Britain out of 'splendid isolation' and signed the Anglo-Japanese Treaty in 1902 with the Japanese ambassador Hayashi Tadasu in London.

With this background, when Lord Harris had written earlier in the year to Count Tadasu informing him about his travels, Count Tadasu had invited Lord Harris to dine at his house. But given the unexpected circumstances, Countess Tadasu, Misao Gamo and Count Tadasu visited the Juzen Hospital. It was during a brief conversation that Count Tadasu slipped in the information that Rash Behari Bose was visiting Japan. The eyes of Count Tadasu and Lord Harris met. Information was exchanged.

As soon as the count left, Lord Harris took his discharge and went to the British consulate. He had to send an important telegram to Madras. Rash Behari Bose was an Indian extremist. And Count Tadasu had hinted that Bose was soliciting support from Japan against Britain.

He was surprised to see Inspector Davies at the telegraph office., and was shocked when he saw what was on the telegram that the inspector held before secreting it into this coat pocket.

'Are you feeling better?' Inspector Davies stammered.

'Yes, thanks, Inspector Davies,' Lord Harris said remaining courteous.

'Have you been discharged from the hospital?'

'Yes,' Lord Harris said and continued, 'I am here to send a telegram to Madras.'

'I am awaiting a phone call from Tokyo,' Inspector Davies said.

'Tokyo?'

'It is with regards to an arrest warrant–'

'For Dr Chettiar?' Lord Harris interrupted.

Before Inspector Davies could answer, he was called.

'Inspector Davies, a phone call from Tokyo.'

Later that evening, Inspector Davies and Lord Harris joined Miss Roberts onboard the *SS Grant.* Although Miss Roberts was under the influence of laudanum, the two lines on her forehead were proof enough that she remained a troubled soul. One of the lines was perhaps Dr Chettiar and the other possibly Lord Harris.

Lord Harris wrote the last line of a sonnet.

'I was the dream, nightmare, demon, and God. I was your worst fear.'

And as he signed his name, he recalled with fear what he had seen on that telegram held by Inspector Davies.

It had read: Lord Harris.

Inside his cabin, Inspector Davies hung his coat that had warrants he had collected from the embassy. Indeed, more than one.

Chapter Nine

---

28 July 1907

Day Thirty-Eight

Macao to San Francisco

On this occasion, Dr Chettiar had his biggest enemy point an Enfield rifle at him. Dr Chettiar was pointing an Enfield rifle at his right temple.

A-Ma behaved as if it was the lovechild between the wind and the ocean, and Captain Burbage was the groom ready to marry her. *A-Ma* did 8–9 knots per hour as it sailed through the Straits of Fo-Kien, which separated China from Formosa. A typhoon arrived but Captain Burbage used the direction of the typhoon to his advantage.

Whilst the world outside was perfect, Dr Chettiar was far removed from it. A typhoon had indeed arrived, and it was in his mind. He felt a heartbeat, but was it from his heart? He struggled to breathe. This was different from that time in the past when he had not seemed to need air to live. He could not sleep. Opium and alcohol had failed him. He could not eat. As every memory emanated from the hidden recess of his cerebrum, his body did not seem to need anything from the world outside. Every page of that memory produced intense pain, and the pain, strangely though, was addictive.

In that

Drop of time

An entrapment

I made love

To that pain of separation from you.

He could diagnose himself as melancholic. He needed to convince himself that he was alive. His mind drifted to that time in the past when she had been present. HRH Kaur.

Back in time

Girton College. She had sat the tripos. HRH Karishma Kaur. Descendent from the lineage of the first Sikh Maharaja, Ranjit Singh.

Dr Chettiar was a student of medicine at Cambridge.

'O my worlds

Bleed my heart

I need more space

For the elixir from your breasts

Inundating my arteries.'

HRH Kaur was dressed in a green of impressionist hues.

Dr Chettiar was dressed in a waistcoat, linen shirt, and trousers. His Panama hat was now being worn by HRH Kaur. They had been punting on the River Cam on that summer's day.

'No, you are angry!' She turned her face away.

'And you are frustrated!' He pointed at her.

'I am not. I am in love with you.' She looked into his deep brown eyes.

'It doesn't feel like that when we are fighting. We are miles away,' he said and sulked.

'Is that what you believe?' She held his face.

'No, we are somewhere together.' He pushed her hands away.

'Where?' she asked.

'Somewhere where there is a clear sky and there are stars,' he said looking at the sky.

'And it was a tiny bit cold so we could huddle into each other.' She sat closer to him.

'And we had just stepped off a carousel,' he recalled.

'We walked up to this guy who was playing the accordion to earn his opium. And you asked him to play our song,' she said.

'And he fumbled with the tunes. Yet we danced,' he said, supporting his chin with his knees.

'You held my waist and then my fingers as I twirled.' She put her arm across his shoulder.

And then they sat silent.

'And that other night; I don't want another night like that ever in our lives,' her voice pleaded.

'Did I kill you?' he asked as he held her fingers.

'No, you were dying and I was pulling you and me from your suicidal act,' she said with her hands on her waist. 'And you apologised.' Her anger dissipated and she continued. 'And you hugged me from behind.'

'Did you hear me say I love you?' he whispered.

'Something you insist you have said ever since I walked into your life.' She held his face.

They anchored at Grantchester.

'You taught me this upside-down thing. Like you do, hanging off the bed,' she said as she bent backwards.

'And you taught me to kiss. And to hug. I am still learning to let you touch my face,' he said as he poured some punch.

'I love watching your face when you sleep,' she said.

'It's nearly time for lunch.' His tummy rumbled.

'Why do we have two plates and two sets of cutlery?' she chided him.

'Don't bite my finger,' he warned her as she nibbled canapes from his hand.

'Your stories distracted me.' She raised her shoulders.

'If we are talking about distractions, how could I ever focus whilst looking at your dimples?'

'That's why I have to blindfold you when we have sex.' She giggled.

'And test the dexterity of my toes,' he said as he got comfortable exploring the depth between her thighs.

'And tie your hands.' She wriggled herself away from him and gently slapped his hands.

'Are you sure?' he asked.

'No, perhaps not. Then you wouldn't be able to hold my throat.' She said little but her bosom said more. 'What's wrong?' she noticed a change in his demeanour.

'Why?' he asked.

'Why are you tugging at your pendent?'

'I have so many things to say sorry about that this lifetime won't suffice,' his voice broke.

'But all that magic you have made would last for several lifetimes too,' she said and embraced him.

'Would you like me to say it?' he asked as they kissed

'What?' she was torn between kissing and speaking.

'I love you.'

'How do you know?' she asked.

'You are scratching my palm,' he said as he kissed her hand.

'You know everything don't you?' She faked being angry.

'That's why sometimes it becomes hard.' He took a deep breath

'You don't need me; you could just live in your head.' She laid her head on his shoulder as the boat was perilously adrift.

Years later, they were stood on the Hungerford Bridge across the Thames. In love but about to separate. Forever. The rain was cold. But as soon as it touched their cloaks, it became fuel and made the fire in their hearts consume their lives.

'No, you are angry!' She turned her face away.

'And you are frustrated!' He pointed at her.

'I am not. I am in love with you.' She looked into his deep brown eyes.

'It doesn't feel like that when we are fighting. We are miles away,' he said and sulked.

'Is that what you believe?' She held his face.

'No, we are somewhere together.' He pushed her hands away.

'In your head. Just in your head.' She was enraged.

'Somewhere where there is a clear sky and there are stars,' he tried.

'So not in this world.' She shook her head.

'In every lifetime,' he pleaded.

'And we lead separate lives?' she said sarcastically.

'Love can never be separated.' He moved so that he could see her face.

'Yet it can be incomplete.' She remained firm.

'I am holding you.' He tried taking her hand.

'From my life!' she shouted.

'We had said that there was no you or me, but us,' he argued.

'You had not, then, said one important thing though.' She pushed him away.

'I have stood by what I said.' He would not give up.

'I have lived a lie believing that we would be married,' she said shocked as reality hit her hard.

'I am a defeated man,' he accepted.

'After you ruined my life.' She punched him and continued, 'After you used me.'

It was the first time he had been punched. It felt deserved. But it was not enough. He needed more, he felt. He needed to be punched more for failing her. Not just today but every day of his life. Every day for the rest of his life as he lived with the guilt of deceiving her and disappointing her. He would wilfully provoke anyone just to be punched; just to be reminded of her last touch even if it had been a punch.

'You have a life to live. A family to have,' he said as he brushed away drops of blood from his nose.

'Don't you dare talk about me.' She was furious at him.

'Please, do not destroy yourself.' He folded his hands and requested.

'You have destroyed me. What do I have left?' She laughed at herself.

'I want to know that you will be happy.'

'I am sure you will be happy now that I am no longer part of your life.' She put her hands inside the pockets of her cloak.

'Love is not enough to live,' was his final response.

Mr Pillai had become used to his master's mental agony ever since the yacht had set sail from Macao. He had heard Dr Chettiar delirious and rambling over events that had possibly happened in the past. Though the words made no sense, suffering did. Love, Mr Pillai recognised. His master would scream and shout. His master would cry and wail. His master would punch and hit. It appeared to Mr Pillai that Poongulali's words had reopened a wound in his master's hitherto hidden heart, and that heart seemed to belong to one HRH Karishma Kaur.

That day, Mr Pillai walked in to find his master ready to commit suicide. He dropped the bowl of rice *konji*, ran to his master, and pulled the Enfield out of his master's hand. Dr Chettiar slapped Mr Pillai.

That was the only time his master had been physically aggressive. Mr Pillai found Dr Chettiar looking at an old paper clip. It was a section of a matrimonial announcement. The clip informed of the wedding of HRH Karishma Kaur to one Count Hein. He could not read what was on the back of the clipping.

Mr Pillai poured a whisky and took it to Dr Chettiar. Dr Chettiar pushed the glass away but grabbed Mr Pillai. And with his tear-filled eyes embraced Mr Pillai. And kissed him. On his lips. Mr Pillai was too stunned to move.

As the seasons feed memories to nature.

I would like to be remembered

Not for piety, not for my wisdom,

But for my appetence for you.

Dr Chettiar saw himself in Mr Pillai's eyes. And came to his senses.

The *A-Ma* sailed under the Golden Gate Bridge in San Francisco just as the *SS Grant* was docking into the harbour.

Chapter Ten

29 July 1907

Day Thirty-Nine

Arrival in San Francisco

On that long omnibus car on eight wheels, with its two rows of seats, sat, well, as per norm, hung Dr Chettiar upside down, in handcuffs. He had not spoken a word since 'they' had boarded at the Oakland station on the Pacific Rail Road that ran 3786 miles from San Francisco to New York, ocean to ocean. Who were 'they'? Mr Pillai, Miss Roberts, Lord Harris, and Inspector Davies.

Dr Chettiar's meditation was disrupted by gunshots and a by a bullet that grazed past his temple.

The passengers from the *A-Ma* and *SS Grant* disembarked on the floating quay with worm-eaten planks. San Francisco.

Lord Harris had indicated that they would be resting at the International Hotel for the train was not due to leave until six in the evening from the Californian capital. He was about to hire a carriage for a charge of three dollars when suddenly Miss Roberts shouted, 'Dr Chettiar!'

It was the first time she had uttered a word since offering her deposition to Inspector Davies. Inspector Davies turned to look at her and then followed her eyes.

On the other side of the road, Captain Burbage, having completed the journey in record time, was bidding farewell to Dr Chettiar and Mr Pillai.

Even before Dr Chettiar could discern whether he was experiencing a hallucination or not, a blow landed on his face. Lord Harris had knocked him down to the pavement.

'Inspector Davies, arrest this murderer!' Lord Harris roared.

Mr Pillai looked bewildered as he helped Dr Chettiar rise.

'I am arresting you on suspicion of murdering Governor Roberts,' Inspector Davies announced. And handcuffed Mr Pillai.

'What?' Mr Pillai was stunned.

Lord Harris appeared unable to comprehend this action by Inspector Davies.

Dr Chettiar did not react to Lord Harris – why he did not show any emotion but continued staring at Miss Roberts who remained on the other side of the road.

'I am arresting you on suspicion of abetting Mr Pillai and obstructing justice,' Inspector Davies handcuffed Dr Chettiar.

Dr Chettiar had his eyes fixed on Miss Roberts, oblivious to what was happening to him. It was entirely appropriate to question whether he was seeing Miss Roberts or whether he was hallucinating and seeing someone else.

The deceit in the looks

Of the predator and the prey.

As I look for that gland that is the receptacle of ambrosia.

And you look for the magnetic nerves that cast a net.

'As for you, Lord Harris. I am arresting you on suspicion of involvement in the murder of Governor Roberts as your gun has been implicated in the murder.'

Lord Harris had now found the answer as to why his name had been on that telegram.

Three warrants. Three handcuffs. The fourth warrant had already been executed on Miss Roberts for the attempted murder of Lord Harris.

'This is absurd,' Lord Harris retorted.

'You will have an opportunity to put your case forward at the Old Bailey,' Inspector Davies replied.

As Inspector Davies later sat in a saloon on Montgomery Street, having a much-needed shave, he tried to assemble the pieces from the jigsaw puzzle in his head. Mr Pillai was the Indian native who had fled from the scene of the murder. Miss Roberts had been a witness. Dr Chettiar and Lord Harris had both arrived at the scene. The gun used for the murder belonged to Lord Harris but had been found in Dr Chettiar's house. They had not denied any of these facts. But they had denied murder. He could not be content with circumstantial evidence but with Lord Harris in a rage, Miss Roberts catatonic, Dr Chettiar in depression and Mr Pillai in neurosis, none had been forthcoming in speaking the truth. He had reconciled to biding his time with the hope that they would open up over the week's journey to New York and the steamer to Southampton.

'Yahi tribes!' a call went out.

Yahi tribes belonged to the Yana group of native Americans, their lands – prior to the invasion by tens of thousands of gold-miners following in the footsteps of James W Marshall – bordered the Yuba and Feather rivers.

The Yana were hunter-gatherers and with the invasion of miners, the deer fled from the crowds, and the mining damaged the streams and supplies of salmon. Further to this, the so-called 'Indian hunter' Robert Anderson launched two raids, which resulted in the brutal massacre of Yahis who were already suffering from starvation and their population reduced to a less than a hundred. They were known for their expertise in bowhunting. Theodore Roosevelt had expressed his prejudice in an 1886 lecture thus:

'I do not go so far as to think that the only good Indians are dead Indians, but as I believe nine out of ten are, and I shouldn't like to inquire too closely into the case of the tenth.'

The train was under attack. The tribes had jumped onto the train. Inspector Davies took the Enfield rifle and started shooting.

'Give me a gun!' Lord Harris shouted. And those were his last words before a couple of marauders broke through the carriage door and knocked him unconscious.

Inspector Davies shot dead one of the marauders but the other man pointed a gun at Miss Roberts whom he used as shield and hostage.

'Leave her alone!' Mr Pillai shouted as the man shot at Inspector Davies. The bullet went through the inspector's right arm. The man dragged Miss Roberts out of the carriage.

'Vellingiri!' Miss Roberts screamed.

My dementia feeds on the words from your mouth.

Not on the silence from your glen.

Dr Chettiar opened his eyes.

'Follow me!' Dr Chettiar shouted at Mr Pillai and went to the carriage door. He laid himself down on the joint between the carriages. He positioned the long chain between the cuffs such that it hung onto the rail. Mr Pillai understood and followed suit on the other side. They had to be careful. There was every chance of losing their limbs or lives. As the wheel trundled on the rail, it passed over their chains and broke them free.

'Mr Pillai, you know what to do,' Dr Chettiar said.

Mr Pillai smiled. He climbed onto the roof of the carriage and immediately had to duck to dodge a bullet.

'Do not stop the train at any cost,' Dr Chettiar ordered him.

Mr Pillai turned to look at his master.

Absence of what is more painful?

Your heart or your hearth? Is it the absence of Time or Space?

Dr Chettiar promised. 'New York or Calais, I will come…'

'For me,' Mr Pillai completed and started running on top of the carriages. He kicked another intruder and pushed him down off the train. He leapt from one carriage to another until he reached the engine.

'I am going to take your revolver and gun,' Dr Chettiar said to Inspector Davies who was using his belt as a tourniquet around his injured arm.

'You are under arrest and you cannot do that,' insisted the inspector.

'I am not asking for your permission,' Dr Chettiar replied as he snatched the weapons and filled his pockets with as much ammunition as he needed. He went to Lord Harris, poured whisky on his face, and sat him up.

'When you feel better and that better be soon, go to the engine room, assist Mr Pillai, and make yourself useful,' he said. He smiled and added, 'The race to Madras is still on,' as he shot at the chain to free Lord Harris. 'Inspector Davies, I am going to rescue Miss Roberts. Good to meet you,' he said to Inspector Davies.

'I will not let you go,' the inspector said as he pulled to him a rifle that was on the floor.

Dr Chettiar though briefly then nodded in agreement. 'Fine, come with me.'

They took it in turns to shoot at the marauders as they jumped out of the train. They ran to the horses that had lost their riders and mounted them. They started following a trail.

As Mr Pillai operated the train instead of the engineer who had been shot dead, he saw the horses disappear. A man dressed in a captain's uniform walked in with a gun pointed at Mr Pillai. Mr Pillai wondered if he had time to explain to the captain that he wasn't a marauder but he was helping by running the train.

A shot was fired.

Lord Harris, had fired that shot. The bullet shattered the gun that the captain was holding. Lord Harris jumped from the top of the carriage into the engine room's compartment.

'I will not let anyone interfere in my race around the world,' he declared.

Mr Pillai shook his head and smiled. 'Dr Chettiar preferred your stiff competition,' Mr Pillai commented as he accepted a swig of whisky from the hip flask that Lord Harris pulled out of the captain's jacket. As he spotted the calamity awaiting them, however, Mr Pillai shouted, 'Lord Harris!' Far ahead, a railway bridge that ran over a valley had all but disappeared but for the poles at either end.

Mr Pillai applied the brakes.

'What shall we do?' Lord Harris asked.

'I know what Dr Chettiar would have said,' Mr Pillai replied.

Lord Harris felt an innate admiration for Mr Pillai. Dr Chettiar would not have picked a rookie in his team. He envied Dr Chettiar.

'What would the bastard have said?'

Dr Chettiar would not talk. He was on a mission and he had to save Miss Roberts. Inspector Davies felt exhausted and dehydrated. Dr Chettiar had bandaged the wound on the inspector's arm, having sterilised it with whisky.

Inspector Davies wondered whether this act of following a trail was part of Dr Chettiar's elaborate ruse to disappear into the Western wilderness. Would he harm Miss Roberts if they did find her? Was he enabling Lord Harris and Mr Pillai to escape? Would Dr Chettiar kill him?

'Inspector Davies, we should find the gang in less than a mile,' Dr Chettiar said as he stood up from examining hoof prints.

'Bloody natives!' Inspector Davies swore.

'Inspector Davies, I had assumed you were a clever man but you have lost my respect.'

'What do you mean?' the inspector asked.

'The Yahi tribes were decimated in 1871 when four cowboys trapped and killed that last thirty in Kingsley cave. These people who raided the train were lawless settlers. You will find that the man who appeared innocent and shouted that it was the Yahis was actually part of the raiders. He would have hoped to get down unnoticed at Omaha to re-join the raiders. I am sure that between Mr Pillai and Lord Harris, they would have captured that criminal dressed in a captain's uniform,' Dr Chettiar said.

Inspector Davies looked ashamed of himself.

Dr Chettiar continued.

'If I were to fall in the skirmish we are about to have with this gang, please take Miss Roberts to safety and concede my defeat to Lord Harris. He deserves Miss Roberts and the success.' He paused and added, 'For the record, neither Mr Pillai nor I murdered Governor Roberts.'

Then, they saw the marauders. Miss Roberts was being carried on a horse with her hands tied.

'Are you ready, Inspector Davies?'

The veteran officer cocked his gun.

It took forty-four seconds. Between Inspector Davies and Dr Chettiar, they shot fourteen bullets. Nine found their marks. Three from Inspector Davies killed.

'I don't believe in killing,' Dr Chettiar said as he apprehended the leader of the gang. 'So, this is what I am going to do,' he said and made the survivors dig holes for themselves and buried them up to their necks.

Inspector Davies sprayed water on Miss Roberts' face. As she regained consciousness, she looked at Dr Chettiar.

As I crawl to a mirage

My eyes do not have to answer this existential question.

They are dead from dehydration during the day

From the scorching heat of your bosoms.

They are dead in the night

Sunk in the deep succour of your bosoms.

And she fainted. They started riding to the nearest town. Inspector Davies still on guard and wondering when Dr Chettiar would attempt to escape.

The train rolled back. And then forward. And gathered pace. Mr Pillai pushed the throttle down as much as it would lend. Lord Harris clung to the railings in the guard's carriage. The train approached the precipice and passed the poles.

'This is on you, Dr Chettiar!' Lord Harris shouted.

Mr Pillai smiled to himself. 'Of course, we can fly!'

When Alberto Santos-Dumont heard the story from Dr Chettiar about his race around the world and the current predicament in reaching New York in time for his ship to Calais, he asked, 'Dr Chettiar, would you like to fly?'

Alberto Santos-Dumont, a Brazilian from a wealthy family of coffee producers had dedicated himself to aeronautics and had won the Deutsch de al Meurthe Prize in 1901 for a flight around the Eiffel Tower. He was now touring America and raising funds to develop his 14-bis. Brazilians, in future, would contend that he had preceded the Wright brothers in demonstrating a practical aeroplane.

'Dirigible!' Dr Chettiar exclaimed when the tarpaulin was pulled back.

After that meeting, Dr Chettiar went to meet Inspector Davies to negotiate a pragmatic plan.

'Inspector Davies, I can find out the truth for you,' Dr Chettiar offered.

'Or will you construct a truth for me, your version?' Inspector Davies remained suspicious.

'I can treat Miss Roberts.' Dr Chettiar offered his services.

'And what do you expect in return?'

'I do not want this race to be interrupted. Please send a telegram to Scotland Yard, Madras, and *Augusta Victoria* that Lord Harris and Mr Pillai are innocent and that their journey should not be impeded.'

'How are you so sure about their innocence?' Inspector Davies asked.

'Lord Harris is my rival, but a gentleman. As for Mr Pillai he may have been conservative with facts, but not because he is a murderer' Dr Chettiar pleaded.

'Are you a murderer, Dr Chettiar?' Inspector Davies was relentless.

'The only time I had to kill was on board the *SS Galia* and in self-defence,' Dr Chettiar conceded.

'If neither of them killed Governor Roberts then who did?' Inspector Davies was after answers.

'We can find out together.' Dr Chettiar remained hopeful.

'Even if it was you?'

'You can stay with me all the way to Madras. If we haven't solved it by then, you can still arrest any of us,' Dr Chettiar promised.

'Lord Harris and Mr Pillai may escape *en route.*' Inspector Davies remained sceptical.

'Lord Harris would put defeating me ahead of anything else in his life. As for Mr Pillai, he will have to come back to Madras.'

'Why?'

Dr Chettiar smiled and drifted into poetry.

'Those who read what is left of my verses

Can, perhaps, imagine you.

But only my lust can make them see you.'

As Lord Harris and Mr Pillai boarded the *Augusta Victoria* bound for Southampton from New York, Lord Harris was grieving for Miss Roberts, uncertain if she was still alive.

Thy walk with me on a cobblestone bridge

The babble of the brook beneath more sensible than words on thy lips

Thy look at the blue sky with the summer sun

The drop of cloud smaller than worries in your heart

Thy led to a garden with a variety of flowers

More in number are the lesser revered leaves green and yellow, as the questions in your mind

And beyond the garden is a muddy path

Which held a memory of June showers

Damp are the tears you hold in thine eyes

There as a silhouette is thy house,

Just as the image of himself in thy soul.

The world outside, beautiful, yet testing thy emotions.

The world inside a shadow yet adding hope to thy love.

I never had a home for I lost my love and with it my heart forever just not now.

Sometime later, the passengers on the *Henrietta,* belonging to the Periere French Transatlantic Company, bound for Calais, witnessed a rare spectacle of a dirigible crash landing on the Hudson and the occupants inside the dirigible rescued by the crew of the Henrietta.

Chapter Eleven

11 August 1907

Day Fifty-Two

London

Lords Cricket Ground. Middlesex were playing Kent. Bosanquet, the master of spin and the inventor of the googly, had a stranglehold on the Kent batsmen. It was the last day of the test. Kent had to score 295 and they had seven wickets in hand. The leather was old. And Bosanquet had taken a wicket from the very first ball of that morning. Cleanly bowled.

Another Kent batsman walked to the crease and took guard. It was part of a challenge. Bosanquet bowled. The defensive stroke failed. A silly point raised a shout. This was followed by half-a-dozen fielders around the batsman and Bosanquet. If the umpire called out, the challenge was lost. The crowd who came to witness that rare spectacle would have been disappointed. The umpire took his time. And shook his head in the negative. 'Not Out! Play!'

'Lord Harris!' one of the stewards rushed to the chair on the deck where the Lord was sat lost not in thoughts but lost in love and life.

He was waiting for thyself.

Thy unaware.

He wanted to see thy face in surprise.

Like the first time thy body would have matured lust. And at a different moment, thy heart would have experienced love.

He wanted to create that moment when love and lust arrive together as a wisdom of the mind.

He waited. Every breath reminding him he is but a fool. Every beat reassuring him that he's astute.

Thy had gone.

He ran to find thyself. Losing the breath for he was no fool. Beating harder for he was fighting for his love.

Until thy heard him too.

And came running and found him

Succumbed to fate but conquering providence.

Thy embraced him from behind.

That love was.

I waited too. Blind to me thou did pass.

Mr Pillai, who was holding on the rails, turned to look at the steward. The steward held a telegram on a silver plate for Lord Harris to receive and read:

Miss Roberts alive and well with Dr.

There was another telegram:

You are not suspect. Investigation continues.

Lord Harris jumped up in joy. He went to Mr Pillai, whom he had started respecting, and said, 'Miss Roberts is alive, and we are suspects no more.' He called the steward. 'Please bring the finest of your champagne. Two glasses,' he said, looking at Mr Pillai.

'You have been acquitted? Or we have been acquitted?' asked an unconvinced Mr Pillai.

Lord Harris frowned at Mr Pillai and replied, 'We,' before secreting the telegrams quickly into his coat pocket.

That evening, when Lord Harris and Mr Pillai sat at the captain's table for dinner, Lord Harris enjoyed Tchaikovsky's String Quartet No. 1 in D Major. The conversation invariably descended to cricket even whilst Lord Harris attempted to indulge the captain into a conversation that would arouse the captain to sail faster to Southampton.

'The best spinner in the world, Bosanquet,' a Mr Lucas Bacmeister said. He had played for Middlesex from 1899–1904 and was currently writing articles for *The Cricketer*.

'The best spinners are from India.' Mr Pillai rose to the challenge.

'Having played in Bombay and Madras, I tend to agree with Mr Pillai.' Lord Harris offered his opinion.

'I am afraid, you haven't followed county cricket in the last few weeks, Lord Harris,' Mr Bacmeister said as he accepted a port from the captain. 'Bosanquet has been steamrolling any opposition,' he added.

'But perhaps we are talking about English batsmen not used to playing the turning ball?' Mr Pillai queried.

'And Lord Harris, could counter Bosanquet?' Mr Bacmeister was scornful.

'Of course he can. I have heard Dr Chettiar praise him as one of the finest wrist players of spin,' Mr Pillai insisted.

Lord Harris looked surprised whilst his heart was mightily pleased.

'Let's not talk about that scoundrel, Chettiar,' Mr Bacmeister said dismissively. He looked at an enraged Mr Pillai and asked, 'Have you seen Lord Harris bat?'

'I have and I don't doubt Dr Chettiar's opinion either,' Mr Pillai said as Lord Harris looked curiously at him.

'Mr Bacmeister,' Lord Harris said and turned to the opinionated commentator. 'I would take on any spinner, any day, on any ground.' He paused before adding, 'And Dr Chettiar is a gentleman.'

'In that case, would you care to prove me wrong?' duelled Mr Bacmeister.

'How?' asked Lord Harris.

'If the captain sped the ship to Southampton, you would still have a day to play for Kent against Middlesex at Lords,' Mr Bacmeister suggested.

Whilst Lord Harris thought, everyone else looked at the captain who said, 'It is possible to get to Southampton in time for the final day's play.'

'But I am on a race around the world.' Lord Harris hesitated.

'The Boat Mail to Calais leaves only in the evening. You could play at Lords and take the train to Dover from Charing Cross Station in time,' the captain reassured Lord Harris.

'But how could I be part of the playing eleven?' asked Lord Harris.

'Well, I could telegram Kent and Middlesex. You will be in the playing eleven. Kent will have to play with a substitute in the first innings who will not be able to bat,' Mr Bacmeister reasoned.

'Yes, it is possible within the rules of cricket,' Mr Pillai agreed.

'And it would be tremendous publicity for the game. Lord Harris bats to save Kent whilst still on his race around the world!'

Bosanquet bowled the next ball. Mr Pillai watched from the balcony as a special invitee. Lord Harris danced down the pitch and negated the spin. The ball flew over long and on for a six. He swept the ball as well as any batsman from India. At lunch, he was on forty-nine. Middlesex needed 220 more. Bosanquet tried bowling around the wicket. Lord Harris reverse swept him. When the cordon around him was reduced to a slip and wicket-keeper, he was on ninety-five. Kent needed 150. They had four wickets. Lord Harris hooked a bouncer and the ball went over a deep leg for a six. He raised his bat and pointed at the commentary box where Mr Bacmeister was sat. He then raised it at a cheering Mr Pillai. At tea, he was on 146. Kent needed eighty-eight.

On the first over after tea, he hit Bosanquet for four successive boundaries. That was the last time Bosanquet bowled in that match. Later that evening, Kent won by one wicket. Lord Harris remained undefeated on 219.

'Dr Chettiar would have been very proud of you,' Mr Pillai said as they boarded the train for Dover.

'That bastard!' Lord Harris chuckled.

'Well, he has always respected you,' Mr Pillai remarked.

'If that was the case, he has a strange way of expressing it.' Lord Harris remained an atheist.

'He is a strange man.' Mr Pillai was accurate.

'Why does he always have to compete with me?' Lord Harris lit a cigarette and continued, 'After all, this journey around the world was a personal challenge I had set to prove my love for Miss Roberts. Why did he have to contest it?'

'Perhaps to bring out the best in you; perhaps to make you appear glorious in the eyes of Miss Roberts. Wouldn't it be more appealing for you to have defeated Dr Chettiar, the man Miss Roberts has put on a pedestal so to speak, rather than having just gone around the world?' Mr Pillai countered.

Lord Harris remained silent. Was his best in love enough? Enough for Miss Roberts to accept his hand instead of that Dr Chettiar's?

More and all the more. Thy love doth demand.

Mine gives myself though you throw away with your hand.

Chapter Twelve

11 August 1907

Day Fifty-Two

San Francisco to Calais

And this scar has festered, plagued by biddings of separation

My blood can heal my heart if it is where the scar is.

But it is private and needs you as a cure.

Dr Chettiar had an Enfield revolver pointed at him. This time it was held by Miss Roberts.

On day three of the transatlantic voyage, Miss Roberts was on the couch. Dr Chettiar was sat on a chair beside her smoking a Trichinopoly cigar.

'I hated my mother,' she started.

He turned to look at her. This was his second attempt using a new investigatory approach into exploring the depths of the human mind – psychoanalysis, propagated by one Dr Freud from Vienna.

'But I loved him,' her face blushed and blossomed. 'He showed me life. He made me happy. It was simple.' She continued,

'A petal from a flower he would offer me as a reward every time I solved his riddle.' She inhaled that fragrant memory.

Dr Chettiar wrote in his book.

'My lust is worth

It makes your face speak that truth your heart hides.'

'He spent more time with me. Mother envied me,' she said and her arrogant face sparkled with celebratory eyes. 'And when Mother died, I was happy.' She was cold and unremorseful. 'I never felt guilty.' She continued, 'He threw me into a river. I splashed water on him. When I came out, he held a towel and wiped my face. His fingers brushed my lips. I pulled the towel and ran to change behind a tree. He did not turn to look. I was disappointed.' She tugged at a beaded necklace she was wearing. The thread unravelled and the beads fell to the floor. 'That hurt in my mind was removed by the hurt he offered my body. It was ecstasy.' She regressed in her manner to an innocent child as she recounted it and jumped on the couch.

'And then I found him doing the same with Vic, my older sister,' she said, now sat on the floor with her head resting on the couch and her face flooded with tears. Her fingers turned in to claws as she scratched that velvet cushion. 'How I wished she was dead!' she sobbed and continued, 'And the following morning, she had died!' She paused and looked at Dr Chettiar. 'What had I done?' she wailed. 'I watched him strangle her as I remained hidden under the cot. When he found out that I knew, he said that it would be our little secret,' she stammered. 'I was enraged. I shouted. I screamed. I stabbed his hand with the knife that was on the table.' Her hand reached out.

'He hit me and I collapsed. When I woke up, I was in a hospital. Apart from a morbid feeling, I could not recall anything about this time, until …' her voice faded.

'Repression,' Dr Chettiar wrote in his diary. Just as Dr Freud had theorised. Repression, that primitive defence mechanism that blocked memories from the conscious mind, yet, the id-ego conflict remained unresolved. She had been stuck in the phallic phase of psychosexual development.

'And all that came flooding back that evening at the Madras Cricket Club.' She looked firm. 'HRH Nachiyar and I were there on our mission. Although we had dealt with the pimp, we wanted that perverse procurer to be brought to justice. So, that boy who was already promised by the pimp was to be our bait. And that boy was brought in by –'

'Mr One Too-Many.' Dr Chettiar broke his silence.

'You knew?' Miss Roberts looked at him with suspicion.

'I found out from a man called Kalingarayan who attempted to kill me.'

She moved to Dr Chettiar and embraced him, kissed his face and neck, and felt for his chest.

'Are you fine? Are you?' She wouldn't stop.

He held her hands and took her back to the couch. He poured a glass of whisky and offered it to her.

'Yes, and that beast came. And with him, walked in my memories.' She threw the glass against the cabin wall. 'I had been twelve then, and he was my father!' She broke down.

This time Dr Chettiar held her. When she raised her head to look up at him, he flicked his finger in front of her eyes and she lapsed into a hypnotic trance.

The following morning when she woke up, she felt reborn.

'Good morning, gentlemen,' she said to Inspector Davies and Dr Chettiar as they were having breakfast.

'Miss Roberts, many thanks for your help,' Inspector Davies said.

She appeared puzzled.

'Yes, Dr Chettiar was just informing me about what you had seen at the murder of Governor Roberts,' he added.

'Pardon me, Miss Roberts, I had to override the confidentiality clause as it involved a crime.' Dr Chettiar bowed.

'When we dock at Calais, I have to send a telegram to Madras for Mr One Too-Many to be arrested for the murder of Governor Roberts,' Inspector Davies informed her.

'That man, Mr One Too-Many, deserves to be shot. And poor Governor Roberts when he found out about that exploitation ring, had decided to expose Mr One Too-Many and that was when Mr One Too-Many decidedly shot and murdered Governor Roberts,' Dr Chettiar finished the story in haste.

Later that evening, Miss Roberts pointed the Enfield revolver at Dr Chettiar during their session.

'Please, tell me the truth,' she bargained with him.

'The truth, Miss Roberts, is that the revolver you are holding has no bullets in it.' He smiled.

Henrietta docked at Calais.

Chapter Thirteen

12 August 1907

Day Fifty-Three

Calais

Platform, Calais station.

The punch landed on Dr Chettiar's face, again. He let go of Miss Roberts who was hugging him and fell to the floor. He took his time getting up, perverse in savouring the pain that brought back memories.

'Stay off her!' Lord Harris shouted.

Mr Pillai ran towards Dr Chettiar.

Miss Roberts pushed away Lord Harris and bent down to look at Dr Chettiar.

At the same time, Mr Pillai hurled himself at Lord Harris. The Calais train station had never before witnessed such a skirmish. The platform was busy with passengers trying to get on, porters hauling cargo, along with sacks of mail, waiting to reach the hands of colonial officers in the East.

If my fingers can transcribe the desires

At the speed of the mind, which translates the dreams of the eyes

Then you can be pleased that I have evolved.

Did it really matter who said that? Or about whom?

Lord Harris rushed at Mr Pillai.

Mr Pillai unsheathed a French Boarding sabre from an onlooker.

'Are you challenging me to a duel, Mr Pillai?' Lord Harris asked in surprise.

A British Hussar threw a *kilij* of Turkish manufacture to Lord Harris.

Mr Pillai pushed Lord Harris to step back and on to the carriage. Sparks flew. More from their eyes than from the sabres. Miss Roberts helped Dr Chettiar stand up.

In the day, your love

Feeds me with poison from your naked breasts.

In the night

I stab you with an unsheathed sabre.

Lord Harris swung from the carriage door and pulled him onto the roof of the carriage.

'Stop!' Dr Chettiar shouted at them.

Mr Pillai jumped to the top of the carriage and with his brute force knocked Lord Harris down.

My lust for you in the morning

Is lonely, disgruntled, inaudible, a thought in mind.

As a feeling in the heart at noon.

And an uncontrollable rebellious act in the swathes of skin in the evening.

Lord Harris punched Mr Pillai's face and tried removing the sabre off him. Mr Pillai landed a kick on Lord Harris's face. Lord Harris slipped off the carriage and fell onto the sacks of mail that were waiting to be loaded onto the train.

Mr Pillai jumped down.

Lord Harris threw a sack at him.

Mr Pillai lost his balance.

Lord Harris jumped on top of Mr Pillai and slapped him. That knocked the turban off Mr Pillai.

Lord Harris felt a blow on his back. Dr Chettiar stood with the bayonet of a rifle pointing at him. Lord Harris went for the sabre that Mr Pillai had.

They traded blows whilst Mr Pillai attempted to get up.

Miss Roberts ran to them. She took the Turkish *kilij*.

They had their weapons pointing at each other.

'Stop this mayhem!' she ordered.

Dr Chettiar turned towards Miss Roberts.

Lord Harris thrust his sabre and ripped off a chain that hung from Dr Chettiar's neck. Instead of a pendant, it held a ring. Before Dr Chettiar could react, Lord Harris caught the ring, knelt in front of Miss Roberts, and asked her, 'Will you marry me?'

Miss Roberts stared at Dr Chettiar. Dr Chettiar was looking at Mr Pillai. And Mr Pillai was gazing at Lord Harris, his hair down to his shoulders, the blood oozing from a cut across his chest, and eyes brimming with tears. He stood not as a man but as a lady. HRH Senbaga Valli Nachiyar.

That was when Dr Chettiar realised that Mr Pillai, alias HRH Senbaga Valli Nachiyar had fought not out of loyalty to his/her master Dr Chettiar, but out of a newfound transatlantic love for Lord Harris.

Let my lust for you age, not rot.

My eyes drown in the tears,

My forehead disintegrates into the ridges.

Dr Chettiar looked at the sky and then at the ring that was now on Miss Roberts' ring finger. He walked to HRH Senbaga Valli Nachiyar.

'Two is company, they say,' he commented and she held his arm and rested on his shoulder.

The train to Brindisi had a carriage for twenty-two passengers including the guard. It left Calais just about half-past one in the morning. It would arrive in Brindisi in forty-eight hours. The carriage was a Pullman Palace and the stateroom was occupied by Lord Harris and Miss Roberts, the newly engaged couple.

Dr Chettiar, HRH Nachiyar, and Inspector Davies occupied three of the berths in a carriage that smelt of smoke. By the time the train arrived at Modena, HRH Nachiyar had given her version of the story.

Miss Roberts and HRH Nachiyar had been friends since Miss Roberts had returned from her studies in Cambridge. Once they had caught the pimp, they had schemed to use the event at the Madras Cricket Club to trap the leader of the sex-trafficking ring. Mr One Too-Many was their prime suspect. At the suggestion of Miss Roberts, she had dressed as a man to enter the Madras

Cricket Club. At this point, Inspector Davies intervened. 'And, yes, of course, Governor Roberts found about Mr One Too-Many and when he confronted Mr One Too-Many, the latter shot him dead. I have sent a telegram to Madras, with an order to arrest Mr One Too-Many. He should be arrested by the time the train arrives at Brindisi.'

When he finished, HRH Nachiyar looked at Miss Roberts and together they stared at Dr Chettiar who broke the silence by asking, 'So what happened after Miss Roberts fainted seeing her father shot dead?'

HRH latched on to his lead and continued, 'I carried Joanna to Lord Harris's carriage for I knew he was…' she hesitated to say the words 'in love with Miss Roberts.'

'Lips close. Language closer.

How long will thy wait to kiss, this composer?' Lord Harris recited from his sonnet.

'For I knew he was … travelling around the world. I thought Joanna would be away from the wretched situation and it would be a relief for her.'

Dr Chettiar looked at HRH Nachiyar. He listened to her eyes and not her lips.

'And then I had to knock off Mr One Too-Many so that he would not do anything to Miss Roberts. Later I realised, I had to join this journey to keep an eye on Miss Roberts and ensure that she remained safe. Hence, I paid a visit to Dr Chettiar. But he had made it complicated by saying that he would not set foot on British territory.'

'Did I learn?

My mind in lust was then foolish.

And now my heart in love is foolish,' Dr Chettiar read from his translation.

'So, what happens when we reach Brindisi?' Lord Harris asked Dr Chettiar.

'Yes, though the Suez Canal is neutral, Port Said in Egypt is part of the British Protectorate and Aden is a British colony,' Inspector Davies added.

'The race continues,' Dr Chettiar was nonchalant in his declaration.

'I do know what is going to happen though when we reach Brindisi,' Lord Harris said with his eyes sparkling.

'We are getting married,' Miss Roberts announced.

'Congratulations!' Inspector Davies rejoiced as Dr Chettiar looked at the poignant HRH Nachiyar.

When you walk away from the cadaver,

My poems are auctioned to be bought by an illiterate to praise his love.

'Will you be my bridesmaid?' Miss Roberts asked HRH Nachiyar.

'Dr Chettiar! This is not the time to fight. You will be my best man,' ordered Lord Harris.

Under the 1836 Marriage Act, at two o'clock in the morning, in a registrar's office in Brindisi, the Italian registrar, woken up with exaggerated pride at becoming just aware of playing a minimal yet crucial part in this race across the world, Lord Harris married Miss Roberts.

Thy walked on a path different to him.

He never walked; he ran or flew.

Then thy saw him. Went to him and said

Thy will walk into his life.

Thy went far. He spent slow.

He wouldn't start. Thy broke down.

When thy crossed him, life would never wait.

He would turn. Thy would progress straight.

Thy would falter. He would be audacious.

He would crash. Thy would cruise.

Until.

Thy rested. He settled.

He found himself in thyself.

Thy lost thyself in him.

Thy held him.

He carried thyself.

Love, that orbit.

Life, together I writ.

It was in 1870 that P&O added Brindisi to its route; it was a major port on the Adriatic coast for trade with Greece and the Middle East. Brindisi meant the head of a deer. The wedding feast at that time of the day consisted of *petiole*, a fried yeast dough stuffed with cod or anchovy, or even the vegetarian option of cauliflower, along with *patani tajedda,* rice and mussels, and the guests were hydrated with almond milk and limoncello.

Inspector Davies returned from the telegraph office and informed them that, 'Mr One Too-Many was transferred to Aden but he has not arrived in Aden since leaving Madras.'

Inspector Davies and Lord and Lady Harris set off to the port to board the Victoria bound for Madras. Its first stop would be Alexandria.

Dr Chettiar and HRH Nachiyar looked at the thing in front of them as they stood outside the entrance to the port. Dr Chettiar read a note that read, 'Thrilled to be part of your adventure. Made to exact measure as you had requested based on my book. With best compliments, Jules Verne.'

A balloon, and, of course, in French tricolour. Made with Lyons silk, yet strong, and coated with *gutta-percha.* The silk doubled at the upper extremity of the oval to buffer the strain. The car, circular, made of wicker-work, and strengthened with iron, weighed 250 lbs. The balloon itself was filled with hydrogen, which was fourteen-and-a-half times lighter than air. This magnificent travel machine was baptised the *Passepartout.* The wicker in addition to a barometer had a thermometer, altazimuth, compass, sextant, chronometer, provisions that included tea, biscuits, salted meat, brandy, opium and two tanks of water. It was calibrated to hold two passengers roughly estimated to weigh as much as Dr Chettiar and HRH Nachiyar combined.

As the Victoria left Brindisi, Lady Harris was astounded at the sight of a balloon flying so close, with Dr Chettiar fiddling at the controls miserably and the balloon colliding with the ship several times. She could bear no more and when the balloon came just above the deck of the Victoria, Lady Harris looked briefly at her newlywed husband and said, 'Please forgive me,' and ran to catch the silken ladder hanging off the balloon and climbed up.

Dr Chettiar was stunned but HRH Nachiyar realised that the balloon was not made for three passengers. She jumped out of the balloon and onto the deck of *the Victoria.*

That was my love, sparrows, a family

And that one egg that fell and broke before it hatched, was my love, me.

Lord Harris waved at his wife.

As I am stranded and in thirst,

The ocean of salt reminds me of your hate.

Chapter Fourteen

26 August 1907

Day Sixty-Seven

The Indian Ocean

Mr One Too-Many was pounding flesh. Every time he hit the depths, he reviewed his options in the light of facts. Kalingarayan's attempt on the train from Egmore to Tuticorin had failed. The SS Galia had returned to Tuticorin from Macao, and he had heard that Kalingarayan was dead. There was every possibility that Kalingarayan might have confessed. Although he had handed that Enfield revolver, found in Dr Chettiar's house, to the police commissioner, thus making Dr Chettiar the prime suspect in the murder of Governor Roberts, he had heard rumours that Inspector Davies had further questions. He had also come to know that Miss Roberts was alive and travelling with Lord Harris. He wondered what she had told Lord Harris. That left his position insecure and his life vulnerable.

He wondered if his customers in the higher echelons of Madras would come to his rescue or offer him up as a scapegoat should this investigation expand beyond the murder of Governor Roberts. He felt uneasy. He felt unsafe in Madras. He continued pounding at the flesh but nothing happened. Then it hurt. Then it shrivelled. He felt that flesh belittle him. He faked an orgasm. The flesh seemed to laugh at him. His hands went for her neck.

The following morning, Mr One Too-Many went to his superior officer and requested a transfer. The request was written on currency and signed in exchange for women. He obtained a transfer order to the British colony of Aden located on the eastern approach to the Red Sea.

The British presence in Aden had commenced in 1796 at the invitation of the Sultan, and in the 1830s the governor of Bombay, Sir Robert Grant, had believed that Hindustan could only be protected by having strong garrisons in places such as Aden on the trade routes that involved the Indian Ocean. In 1838, Muhsin bin Fadl ceded seventy-five square miles including Aden to the British, and the British East India Company landed Royal Marines to secure Aden on 19 January 1839. Aden became an important coaling station equidistant from the Suez, Bombay, and Zanzibar.

But these were not the reasons why Mr One Too-Many requested a move to Aden. He had realised that nowhere in the British Kingdom would be safe for him. Aden was a gateway to the Trucial Coast, thus named since the General Maritime Treaty of 1820. Previous to this, it was also known as the Pirate Coast. Although the treaty had offered protection to British vessels, it did not stop the coastal wars between the tribes and so the pirate raids continued intermittently. Such raids were also triggered by religious upheavals in Central Arabia, and when the British opted to focus on supporting the slave trade in East Africa, trade vessels and steamers in the Persian Gulf became vulnerable to piracy.

Barut was captain of one such pirate vessel, the *Al Kahila.* The *Al Kahila* was docked in Madras and he was awaiting trial on charges of acts of piracy.

The day that Governor Roberts was murdered, Mr One Too-Many had visited Governor Roberts at the request of Kalingarayan to request leniency on the sentencing of Barut. Barut had provided exotic pleasures to the elite of Madras through his nexus with Kalingarayan and Mr One Too-Many. Subsequent to visiting Governor Roberts, Mr One Too-Many had paid a visit to the man in prison. He had bargained with Barut, but it had not been restricted to monetary rewards for releasing him from prison. There was more to it.

The day that Barut escaped from the central jail in Madras, and the *Al Kahila* had disappeared from the Madras dock, Mr One Too-Many was reported on the official record as having boarded a steamer to Aden.

In truth though, he was with Barut on the *Al Kahila*, as an equal shareholder, having arranged for the vessel to be recognised as a 'friendly Arab vessel' with a document that would name it *nacoodah*, the official permit for the vessel to trade in the Arabian Peninsula and the Indian Ocean.

And so, it came to be that on one of his sojourns as he looked through his telescope, Mr One Too-Many saw a P&O steamer, the Victoria. It was time to hunt.

CHAPTER FIFTEEN

28 August 1907

Day Sixty-Nine

The Indian Ocean

From the balloon, Dr Chettiar was staring at an 8m cannon. There was sky above and sea below.

As birth and death

The pain in your heart and the pleasure in your bosoms.

Passepartout. The barometer on the balloon rose by two inches as they reached an altitude of 1500 feet. Lady Harris was an expert in the art of placing the balloon in currents best adapted to the final destination of Madras and making it ascend or descend by dilating or contracting the gas in the balloon through the application of different temperatures. This mechanism relied on the circulation of oxygen and hydrogen, using a network of pipes from gas cylinders.

Dr Chettiar poured a brandy and offered it to Lady Harris.

Such a tranquil moment

When you made me realise my selfishness.

In loneliness, I write!

In lust, I write!

They looked at the idyllic sky with its myriad hues.

'Thank you for providing me with this opportunity,' Lady Harris said as their cups touched.

'Lady Harris, I did not offer you this opportunity. As you recall, you jumped on to the balloon and poor HRH Nachiyar had to jump out to ensure we manage the balloon's load.'

Let us try telling the story again!

So, He created you and me.

You asked me for the apple.

I informed him.

He crossed me and went to obtain that apple to woo you.

The serpent bit him to death! Who is the God?

'I should be the one thanking you for taking this risk to keep this balloon and me safe. Not to mention the ordeal you will face in placating Lord Harris,' Dr Chettiar said.

'Dr Chettiar.' She smiled as she stood by his side. Her face would one moment, stare into the future, and in the next, stare into his eyes in the present. 'I am not naïve enough to believe that you could not control this balloon. It was an act for the world to be fooled,' she said.

Dr Chettiar pushed his glasses down from his forehead to his eyes.

'What are you trying to hide, Dr Chettiar?' she asked.

'Well, you kept your love for Lord Harris hidden for a long time,' he batted back.

'Joanna, please, for old time's sake,' she insisted and continued, 'I had kept it hidden from myself. I was worried that like all things in my life I would destroy that too.' She turned to face the horizon that no longer showed her future but was a curtain for her traumatic past.

'You continue to look worried,' Dr Chettiar observed.

'I am worried. I am worried that I will destroy Edward,' she confided in him.

'No one can destroy anyone, Joanna.' Dr Chettiar was philosophical.

The fire that is created by the friction between our nerves

Can ruthlessly consume those same nerves when we are alone.

Threatening clouds looked nearer than before.

'Shouldn't we ascend?' Dr Chettiar asked.

'You didn't answer my question,' Lady Harris persevered.

'I am no Lord Harris to fall in love, Joanna'

'But you are a Vellingiri to die in love?' she asked.

'You would make a very determined therapist,' Dr Chettiar said as he poured brandy into his cup.

Lady Harris increased the temperature on the gas cylinder that dilated the balloon and got them up to 3000 feet.

Just as my presence bore out the juice from your deep darkness

My absence pumps out tears from your shallow luminescence.

'I thought–' Lady Harris started.

'Are you now feeling and thinking for me?' he interrupted her.

'Shouldn't I?'

He held her hands. The ring that Lord Harris had cut off his chain was adorning her graceful finger.

'Beautiful, isn't it?' he pointed.

'I selected it. Of course, it would be beautiful.' she smiled.

'Yes, you did. How could I ever forget that?' he shook his head.

'You would never forget in love.'

'That bridge on the River Cam,' he reminisced.

'You were running.' She recalled that day.

'And you were on the punt. I was mad.' He accepted.

'You were in love.' Her eyes moistened.

'And I jumped.' He held her hand tight as he said that.

'And missed the punt.' She laughed.

'And the ring too.' He made a sad face.

'And swam up empty-handed'

'Not quite empty-handed, I would say,' he corrected her.

'Yes, with reeds, and not just on your hand,' she agreed with him.

'Yes, but with a ring made of reeds.' He was proud of himself. 'Hastily knotted as I held the punt.' He enacted the art of making a ring using reeds.

'And you offered it,' she said.

'And it was accepted.' His eyes brightened.

They both laughed nostalgically.

'I was so happy that day,' Lady Harris said as she kissed him on his cheek.

'I was content.' Dr Chettiar finished another cup of brandy.

'Oh, were you?' Lady Harris teased him.

'Wasn't I?' Dr Chettiar looked confused.

'Oh, you were, after this ring reappeared,' she said pointing to the ring on her finger.

'Yes.' He nodded and fondled the ring.

'You had held it all along in your coat pocket'

Dr Chettiar smiled sheepishly. 'And when it ended–'

'Shall we stop there?' Lady Harris stopped him.

'You asked me a question earlier.' He became frustrated.

'I shouldn't have.' She moved away from him.

'Is the answer so hard that you cannot even bring yourself to hear it?' He followed her.

'No, not as hard as living with it as you do.' She held him.

He held her hand tight; his fingers gripping that ring.

'When it ended, I had the ring returned,' he said.

'Thrown back at you. You can be truthful.' She finished reminiscing.

The storm was approaching them.

'We need to ascend even higher,' he said.

The inflammable balloon now had to pass through the zone of fire.

'I am working on it!' she shouted for him to hear since sound was muffled at the altitude they were climbing and the noise from the natural phenomena they were witnessing was deafening.

As they ascended, the phosphorescence produced by the Fires of St Elmo appeared ethereal. She let her eyes off the altazimuth. They ascended rapidly to 12,000 feet.

'When I heard you say at the Madras Cricket Club that you were going around the world,' Lady Harris started as Dr Chettiar refilled her cup with brandy. 'I thought you were going in search of her.'

'I don't have to search for her. She is in my memories. You. Her. Me. Cambridge. Love. Everything.'

That's when she realised that they had ascended too fast. He was struggling to breathe. He fell on her. The giant red full moon looked like a furnace ready to consume them.

He opened his eyes. He saw her.

'Karishma,' he called and held Lady Harris by the throat.

'Let me go,' she gasped for breath. His hands only became tighter than before. She tried to push him away but she could feel the lack of oxygen hitting her ruthlessly. She coughed. Her legs shook.

'Why did you not kill me? This suffering is crueller than death!' he was ranting. His hands continued gripping her throat.

'I am not Karishma,' she pleaded, but she could only hear herself in her head. She looked into his eyes.

In the orbit of your eyes

Union and separation are imposters as victory and defeat.

The red moon closed in on them.

When she woke up, she saw Dr Chettiar on one side. She smiled, happy to be back at Girton College in Cambridge. She turned to the other side hoping to see Karishma, her best friend.

And that was when reality hit her. She pulled herself up. She went to read the altazimuth. They had come down to 8000 feet. She started deflating the balloon and rushed to Dr Chettiar.

'Wake up!' She slapped him. Then listened for his heart and breath.

As I lay on my shadow

My mind can make you vanish in my dreams.

But what can my poor senses prey on in your absence?

She blew air into his mouth. She thumped his chest. She cursed. She cried.

'Don't leave me!' she screamed.

She scratched his face. Opened his eyes. Blew more air. Hit his chest.

And cried again. And hid her face in her thighs.

'Joanna!' he called, his eyes faint and his lips quivering. 'Is Karishma safe?' he asked.

She jumped on top of him and rained a thousand kisses on his face and chest. And then slapped him hard and emptied a bottle of brandy on his face.

'Well, that was some therapy.' He laughed as he regained his consciousness.

'And when you are ready, can you please give me a hand to guide this balloon to Hindustan?' She brought him up to speed.

'Could you find me opium?' he asked.

'I could find you Karishma.' She looked serious.

And after two hours, when they were drifting low on the Arabian Sea, past the Persian Gulf, Dr Chettiar realised that they did not even have time to think. The 8m cannon from a ship fired and set the balloon ablaze.

Those that read what is left of my verses

Can perhaps imagine you.

But only my lust can make them see you.

Chapter Sixteen

14 August 1907

Day Fifty-five

From the Mediterranean Sea to the Arabian Sea

His best-ever words

That God knew and he did, had been when he was but six.

He knew less of language

He knew even less of people

He knew the least of this world.

And then he wrote

A suicide note.

He was ready to kill himself.

In his limited vocabulary

With his infantile cursive writing.

He wrote.

He could never say why.

There was none to believe.

Then he threw the paper into the brook where robins drink.

And days and months and years, he did give

To this world. And everyone

Still would complain even when they did receive.

Now all he wants is to breathe love

Or to die now.

Is that too much to ask of this world?

The world, that only wants him to suffer and die old.

It did not take much for a dream that Lord Harris had to turn into a nightmare. Or perhaps, reality was worse than a nightmare. He restricted himself to his suite. He did not use the bed. He could not sleep. Neither was he awake.

'If you truly wish to find someone you have known and who travels, there are two points on the globe you have but to sit and wait, sooner or later your men will come there: the docks of London and Port Said,' Rudyard Kipling had said.

When the Victoria docked at Port Said, he looked at the sky. She wasn't there. He tried convincing himself by saying that she had married him. But could she not put being with him ahead of being on a balloon? And that too with that Dr Chettiar! But she was going to live with him even beyond death. Yet, what if something befell her on this adventure on the balloon? He would make Dr Chettiar pay for it in more than equal measure. Perhaps he would win this race and settle this rivalry with Dr Chettiar once and for all. But in that case, she would lose and he would live his life with the guilt of defeating her. The answers became questions and such questions had no answers.

HRH Nachiyar, even though she'd found this sudden change of fortune advantageous, pitied the despondent Lord Harris who had chosen to isolate himself in his room. The Victoria docked at Port Said. She had gone out to witness the chaotic world of boatmen trying to board her and stewards whipping them away. Only the chosen few were allowed to carry passengers from the Victoria to the shore.

Once she arrived onshore, she witnessed the haunting performance of a women-only-orchestra. Her hand reached out to hold her love, but it was just air she could embrace. She felt odd that in this journey she had seen Dr Chettiar, who had callous regard for human relationships, become melancholic in remembering his love, and Lord Harris who adored Joanna and worshipped love had become depressed in living love. And there she was, in unrequited love. Perhaps it was true that sadness was the synonym for love. She walked back to the shore, her dress stained with sand, to find boatmen bargaining for a higher fee for a return journey to the ship.

Back on the deck of the Victoria, she found Inspector Davies unhappy with the lamentable performance of a magician.

'There is no magic in life if one works out the meaning,' she teased him as she took his hand.

'The meaning of love?' he asked, being a shrewd observer of human behaviour.

'What do I do?' she asked him.

'You can be stronger for Lord Harris,' Inspector Davies comforted her.

'Do you believe in love?' she asked him as the Victoria set sail on the Suez to Aden.

'It is about your belief, HRH,' Inspector Davies replied.

'I wish Joanna would fly away with Dr Chettiar.' She laughed at her wishful thinking.

'If that were to happen, you would lose Lord Harris too or at the very least what you would then have of Lord Harris would be a man with no heart.' Inspector Davies was blunt.

'Like Dr Chettiar?' she was rhetorical.

Inspector Davies nodded in agreement.

The following morning, the men who had slept on the deck, since women not allowed, were clearing away their mattresses. The women were allowed back on deck only after eight in the morning. HRH Nachiyar walked up to the deck where Inspector Davies was sitting and reviewing his report.

'I have decided,' she said and continued, 'I am going to speak to Lord Harris.'

But it took her for the Victoria to cross Aden to gather the courage to do so and more importantly for Lord Harris to emerge from his isolation. Although he had missed an excursion to the English Club House, he had not failed to notice the beaded necklace HRH Nachiyar was wearing, which she had purchased from a male vendor with three wives and who had bleached his hair like every other native in the settlement.

'Lord Harris,' she said.

'HRH Nachiyar,' he greeted her.

'I am very sorry for–'

Lord Harris interrupted HRH Nachiyar. 'You must forgive me for not attending to you ever since we left Brindisi,' he apologised.

'Please, you do not have to apologise. I understand…'

He turned his face away from her.

She tried again. 'I read your sonnet.'

He looked at her in pain and pleasure.

'It starts like this:

He would meet you in his library

When thy attempt to understand his love, thy would add more sections to his library…'

'*And in that library, I would ask thy hand to marry,*' Lord Harris completed.

'I was moved,' she said.

'Thank You.' He looked pleased.

'Joanna deserves you. She is so much in love with you,' she said.

'Thank you.' He blushed and then added in doubt, 'Do you think?'

'She has always talked about you,' HRH Nachiyar confirmed.

'As a friend?'

HRH shook her head in disagreement and said, 'As her life.'

Lord Harris remained circumspect and asked, 'In what respect?'

'In love,' she replied.

'It means a lot hearing this from you.' Lord Harris looked a different man.

'I envy her.' HRH became candid.

'Why?' He was shocked.

HRH said, 'Because I have fallen in love with you.'

He could not have heard it for a cannon call ripped through the hull of the Victoria.

HRH Nachiyar ducked the sabre but punctured the throat of her attacker with her right index finger. As he fell, she took the sabre that at last had found someone worthy enough to grip it.

Lord Harris punched a pirate. His hand broke the man's orbit as he grabbed his attacker's sabre. Inspector Davies shot from having taken cover behind the mast.

The pirates knew that they would suffer casualties but when they succeeded it would only be those who survived who received the share of their plunder.

Lord Harris looked at the Arab who was giving orders from the pirate ship.

'Can you pass me the rope?' he asked HRH Nachiyar.

She understood his plan. She dodged a bullet, threw a dagger at the pirate who was shooting, did a somersault, and reached for the rope attached to a ring nailed to the railing on the deck.

Instead of passing the rope to Lord Harris, she ran to the end of the deck, holding the rope, thus generating momentum for her to swing herself to the pirate ship.

Lord Harris threw a sabre at a man who was attempting to intercept her path. He saw that as she landed, her legs become stronger than a crocodile's jaws and strangled a pirate on the pirate ship.

Lord Harris raced up to a pirate who had managed to get onto the Victoria and knocked him off the ship. He took his sabre and jumped to the sail, which he slit with the sabre. Holding onto the torn end, he flung himself to the pirate ship.

The Arab threw a dagger at HRH Nachiyar that pierced her thigh as she strangled another pirate. The Arab jumped on her and wrestled her on the deck. Lord Harris ran towards them but his path was intercepted by an Englishman.

'Mr One Too-Many?' he said stunned.

'Welcome aboard the *Al Kahila,*' the man replied and the butt of his carbine knocked Lord Harris out cold. The Arab twisted the dagger into HRH Nachiyar's right thigh as she attempted to throttle him. Just before she fainted, she saw the face of Mr One Too-Many.

When she woke up in the dark galley of the *Al Kahila*, tied, she strained to recognise the bodies; some were alive but many were dead. She identified Lord Harris and Inspector Davies. She tried trusting her eyes. She believed they were alive. When she closed her eyes, she believed they were dead.

They were alive. They too were alive.

Chapter Seventeen

28 August 1907

Day Sixty-Nine

The Indian Ocean

Was it his lips or was it his heart that called my name?

Or was it thy ears or did they hear being called love or life, for then it was one and the same?

Lady Harris opened her eyes sluggishly and saw Lord Harris kick Dr Chettiar's face in the dark galley of the *Al Kahila.*

'Generations in time will make you more beautiful with the interpretation of my verses,' Dr Chettiar said.

'This is no time for poetry!' Lady Harris shouted as they clung to the wicker basket that was descending rapidly into the sea below.

'Hold onto the balloon. It will float!' Dr Chettiar screamed.

'No, the weight of the basket will suck the balloon down with it,' she replied.

They could see the pirate ship that had shot down their balloon cruising towards them. Ropes were thrown towards them from the vessel.

Barut watched as Dr Chettiar and Lady Harris were pulled up.

'Who are you?' Barut addressed them in Persian.

'Dr Chettiar and Miss Roberts!'

Everyone turned in the direction of that voice.

Mr One Too-Many stood in his red coat and breeches along with a black turban tied Persian style.

'Lady Harris' she corrected him with bitterness in her voice. Half-a-dozen sabres and a dozen eyes were ready to devour her. Mr One Too-Many walked up to them, placed his arms across their shoulders, and asked, 'What are you doing with a murderer?'

'What's a murderer doing on a pirate ship?' Dr Chettiar retorted.

Mr One Too-Many slapped him hard and said, 'I have always wanted to do that.'

He held Lady Harris by her face. 'And as for you, Lady Harris.' He cut her lips using his nail and watched as blood dribbled down her chin and onto her bosom.

'A passenger ship with a British flag!' Barut cried. Bells rang.

'Take these two to the galley,' Mr One Too-Many ordered and looked through his telescope.

'They have to be killed,' Barut reminded him.

'I need them alive until they sign a declaration confirming that they killed Governor Roberts. They can be killed later.' As an afterthought, he added, 'But they will have to experience hell first.

The hell that every orphan in the slums of London experiences in their childhoods.'

'Fire!' Barut shouted.

The first volley of cannons struck the Victoria.

They had all been tied together with a long rope and taken to the top deck. The heat of the sun burnt the deep gash on HRH Nachiyar's right thigh.

Lord Harris had a vacant look in his eyes as Lady Harris rested on his shoulder.

Dr Chettiar pointed at Mr One Too-Many and whispered into Inspector Davies' ear, 'He is Governor Roberts' murderer.'

Lady Harris turned to look at Dr Chettiar.

'A reunion.' Mr One Too-Many appeared elated. 'I am sorry that this ambience doesn't quite match that of the Madras Cricket Club.' He bowed.

'I am arresting you on behalf of His Majesty's government–' Inspector Davies started. He couldn't finish his sentence as Barut had slammed a fist in his face.

'It is rude to interrupt,' Mr One Too-Many warned Inspector Davies. 'The last time we were together, Governor Roberts was, unfortunately, murdered.' He paused. 'Perhaps it is destined that I have to avenge his murder.'

'You murdered him!' HRH Nachiyar shouted.

Mr One Too-Many went to HRH pulled her up by her hair, forced open her mouth, and held her tongue.

'Next time you say something, I will cut off your tongue.' He spat on her face and pushed her down.

He produced a piece of paper. 'This document states that you, I mean all of you, conspired to murder Governor Roberts as he had refused the hand of Miss Roberts in marriage to Lord Harris. I want all of you to sign it.' He walked to Inspector Davies and said, 'And you will sign it as a witness.'

He gave the paper to Barut who took it first to Lord Harris.

Lord Harris rammed his head into Barut's knees. As Barut lost his balance, his dagger fell onto the deck.

Barut punched Lord Harris until the latter collapsed. Lady Harris continued staring at Mr One Too-Many. This time, Barut took the paper to HRH Nachiyar.

'Even if I sign this, you are going to kill us,' she refused.

'Of course. See this as a final act of benevolence before your death. What do you say in your religion? A good deed to take you to *Vaikundam*,' Mr One Too-Many said.

'I would prefer to kill you to reach *Vaikundam*!' she replied.

Mr One Too-Many went to Lady Harris. 'What do you think Lady Harris?' he asked her.

She kept staring at him. He held her by her face and kicked away at Dr Chettiar who had tried to pull him down.

'I can see how you trapped your father.' He laughed as his eyes gleamed.

'Stop this!' Dr Chettiar shouted. At the same time, he attempted to kick Mr One Too-Many.

Mr One Too-Many moved and Dr Chettiar kicked the deck instead. Barut bent down and twisted Dr Chettiar's legs.

HRH shrieked in horror.

Dr Chettiar held her gaze.

Her eyes followed his. Initially, it was to his feet.

Mr One Too-Many saw Lady Harris hold her chin up and smile at him as she licked the dry blood on her lips. He moved his hand to her chin and then down to rip off her bodice. As her bosoms were exposed to the elements, Lady Harris remained unflinching.

'You bastard!' Inspector Davies shouted as he scrambled up.

'Enemy spotted!' A siren went off.

'Well, well, it seems to be our lucky day, another ship to plunder. Maybe you, Lady Harris, are our Lady Luck! Maybe I should let you live as a slave on my ship,' Mr One Too-Many said and pushed her down. Her head slammed against the railing.

'It is the Inquilab!' Barut shouted above the noise of the cannon fire.

The Inquilab was a steamer built by W. Pile & Co with a hull length of 2000ft and tonnage of 1054 NRT. She belonged to the flamboyant Dutch count, Piet Hein, who since falling in love with Hindustan and marrying an Indian princess, had taken to philanthropy and the role of protecting the merchant navy in the Arabian Sea from pirates.

Both the ships churned the sea to gain leverage for the cannons to find their marks. A cannon from the Inquilab blasted through the mast of the Al Kahila. A cannon from the Al Kahila set the deck of the Inquilab raging with fire. From that fire, an arrow was shot with a rope attached to it. A valorous crew from the Inquilab was elegant in sliding down the rope and shooting from a revolver simultaneously at the pirates before jumping on to the deck of the Al Kahila.

Amidst the chaos, HRH Nachiyar used her feet to retrieve the dagger that Dr Chettiar had pointed out to her. She cut her hands free and then freed Lord Harris. Barut saw her and thrust his sabre at her. She jumped on him and landed the might of her knees on his abdomen. As he fell, his revolver rolled out of the holder. HRH Nachiyar sat on top of him and, using her fingers, gouged open his chest, slammed her fist through his ribs, and plucked out his heart.

Lord Harris pushed her down to protect her from being hit by a bullet. She held him tight. She was shivering. Her breathing was rapid. She rested her head beneath his chin. A pirate came to cut them but Lord Harris rolled with her and grabbed the sabre that was still in Barut' hand. He deflected the next swipe and still holding onto HRH Nachiyar, thrust his sabre into the pirate's chest.

He then released HRH Nachiyar and went to Lady Harris and covered her with his coat. He cut her free from the rope. HRH Nachiyar freed Dr Chettiar.

Lady Harris saw Dr Chettiar attempt to free Inspector Davies whilst Mr One Too-Many appeared. He aimed his gun at Dr Chettiar. Lady Harris took the revolver that lay beside Barut and as she flung herself over to Dr Chettiar, she shot Mr One Too-Many between the eyes. Mr One Too-Many fired at the same time as Lady Harris.

Lady Harris fell down on Dr Chettiar as the lifeless body of Mr One Too-Many fell into the sea.

Lord Harris reached out for his wife.

The birth pangs of my love are more violent than those of the creation of universes known and unknown

But peaceful compared to the death of my love I mourn.

Dr Chettiar held the lifeless body of Lady Harris.

When the eyes of our senses meet

They create a tremor

The flicker of the wings of a butterfly

That opens your floral lips

Into rhythms and waves of a delicate smile

Unseen, but palpable.

Lord Harris pulled his wife onto his lap.

Inspector Davies sat next to Lord Harris, saying a silent prayer.

HRH Nachiyar wailed.

As the Al Kahila was being destroyed and the pirates were surrendering, the valorous crew from the Inquilab emerged. They brushed off the flames, slashing anyone in their way, and marched up to that man who looked like he had been defeated once again.

'Dr Vellingiri Chettiar!'

Chapter Eighteen

28 August 1907

Day Sixty-Nine

The Indian Ocean

Lord Harris punched Dr Chettiar. 'You let her die!' He swung again at Dr Chettiar but his hand was held back by a firm grip. He turned around to find who was holding him.

The green turban around her head came down her ears as a thin veil. She removed her veil.

'I have not seen myself in such a long time,' Dr Chettiar said, his heart refusing to believe what his eyes were seeing.

'I have been waiting for this moment,' she replied and punched him.

This was no memory of being punched in London on the Hungerford Bridge. It was no flashback either. It definitely was not one of those punches that Dr Chettiar seemed to have relished soliciting over the years.

HRH Nachiyar moved towards Dr Chettiar but she was pulled back by Lord Harris.

'HRH Karishma Kaur,' Dr Chettiar said and bowed as he caught a sabre thrown towards him by HRH Kaur.

'You are angry,' he observed as he took guard.

'And you are frustrated,' she said as she exchanged blows with him. The tip of her sabre made a tiny incision above his left eyebrow.

'I am not,' he denied as he blinked to get his vision back and continued, 'I am in love with you.'

She paused as their sabres intersected, their bodies incendiaries, and their eyes ready to ignite.

'It doesn't feel like that when we are fighting,' she replied and headbutted him.

'Is that what you believe?' Dr Chettiar asked as he regained his balance.

Their sabres clashed again. But this time, Dr Chettiar pushed HRH Kaur to a wooden barrel that was burning. Her face was brighter than the flames. Her blood was warmer than the fire.

'No? Are we somewhere together?' she questioned as she kicked and pushed him away.

'In my heart,' he breathed as he fell down.

It was then that she noticed he had managed to make a cut below her neck.

'A heart that you never had,' she declared, as she made violent slashes that he managed to defend.

'Yes, I don't have it because I gave it to you.' He gasped for breath as he went on his guard again.

'After you had destroyed mine.' She was spiteful.

Dr Chettiar dropped his guard. He stretched his arms to either side and looked up at the sky.

'After I had destroyed myself.' He yielded and threw his sabre away.

She walked to him, her sabre pointing at his chest.

'You won't fight?' she almost pleaded.

'I am fighting but not in a way you would appreciate,' he said, looking away from her.

'Not in love?' she pulled his face towards her.

'Love is not enough to live,' he said as he removed the sabre from her hand.

'Or to die,' she completed.

They stared at each other. In that moment, they seemed to live those years they had but lived with memories.

He stepped back.

'You still do not like your face being touched.' She smiled as he held her fingers and walked her to where Lord Harris was sat with his deceased wife on his lap.

'Joanna!' HRH Kaur wailed for her friend from her years in Cambridge and fell to her knees.

Dr Chettiar walked away whilst HRH Nachiyar attempted to console HRH Kaur.

The lustful earth announces the pain from the long day

In the form of the self-inflicted whip from the tides that get longer in the evening

Inspector Davies lifted Lord Harris and offered him some whisky to drink. But as soon as the lips of Lord Harris touched the flask, he felt sick and vomited. He knelt down and took his wife's lifeless hand and placed it on his cheek. Tears rolled down and fell on the ring she was wearing.

'Ka! Are you fine?' Count Hein asked as he walked across the plank from the Inquilab to Al Kahila.

HRH Kaur wiped away her tears and informed Count Hein about the death of Lady Harris and introduced him to Lord Harris.

Inspector Davies and HRH Nachiyar introduced themselves and thanked the Dutch count for defeating the pirates and saving them. She then called, 'Dr Chettiar!'

He turned back. He had replayed this scene so many times in his head ever since he had parted with HRH Kaur.

'Meet my husband, Count Hein,' she said.

Count Hein walked up to Dr Chettiar and as Dr Chettiar offered his hand, the count punched Dr Chettiar on his face so hard, that Dr Chettiar lost his balance and almost fell off the deck and into the sea.

Count Hein held onto him. 'So, you are the man who cheated on Ka,' he confirmed and as Dr Chettiar looked past the count at Countess Kaur-Hein, the count laughed and said, 'Had you not, I would not have found the most beautiful and loving lady in this world.'

Dr Chettiar embraced Count Hein and said,

'O, Ravana!

The vanquished, the victorious!'

Even though Dr Chettiar had played out this scene thousands of times in his head, never had he imagined that it would be accompanied by words from Lord Harris! Lord Harris had recited that to Dr Chettiar somewhere between Modena and Brindisi.

Thy are in love with him.

Thy love succeeds to disprove the beliefs of your time.

Mine, love that failed, can only find poignant words to rhyme.

That evening, as they sat down for dinner on the Inquilab, Count Hein, having heard the wonderful adventures of the two rivals in their race around the world, observed, 'So, gentlemen, it has come down to the last leg.'

'We should be in Madras by tomorrow evening,' Countess Kaur-Hein announced.

'In seventy-one days,' HRH Nachiyar confirmed.

Dr Chettiar and Lord Harris looked disinterested.

'What would it mean to win?' asked Count Hein.

Inspector Davies looked at them curiously.

'The life I had,' replied a forlorn Lord Harris. He had started this journey with the aim to impress upon Joanna his adventurous character streak. She was his life. And she was no more.

HRH Nachiyar, who sat beside him, held his hand.

Everyone looked at Dr Chettiar.

'I am sorry, this isn't going to sound original, but I would have to say, that it would mean the life I too had,' Dr Chettiar said and stubbed out a cigar. He was missing his favourite Trichinopoly brand.

Count Hein proposed a toast. 'To the lives lived!'

That night Dr Chettiar and Lord Harris stood by the deck.

'Joanna would have been very proud of you,' Dr Chettiar remarked.

'She always held you in high regard, why, even higher than me,' Lord Harris responded.

'Oh, you haven't heard the abuse she hurled at me throughout the time I knew her.' Dr Chettiar chuckled.

'You would have deserved every one of those.' Lord Harris laughed.

'She loved you,' Dr Chettiar said.

'Yet she died for you,' Lord Harris, in pain, struggled to complete his sentence.

'No. She did not die for me. She had to kill Mr Too-Many. Thanatos. Her past had to die thus.' Dr Chettiar offered an explanation.

Lord Harris looked intently at Dr Chettiar. 'Why have you always fought with me?'

'Because you are the best man I have ever known,' Dr Chettiar conceded.

'You don't mean it though, do you?' Lord Harris said doubtfully.

Before Dr Chettiar could answer, HRH Nachiyar appeared on deck and ran up to Dr Chettiar. She punched him.

'Just like he did not mean his love for Karishma!' she shouted as Lord Harris held her back.

'You lied to her. You were married!' she continued ranting. She had just finished speaking to Countess Kaur-Hein. 'You have never known love. You were unfaithful to your wife and you betrayed Karishma. Poongulali was correct!' She did not stop.

Dr Chettiar poured whisky over his face.

'You don't have an answer, do you?' she persisted.

'No,' Dr Chettiar said. He slid down and sat with his back against the railing. He smiled at HRH Nachiyar and said, 'You are correct, as are Poongulali and Karishma.'

Her eyes softened. She knelt down to him and begged, 'Please, say I am wrong.'

'You believe more in me than I ever believed in myself.' He rested his head on her shoulder and added, 'Or that anyone ever believed in me.' He then looked at Lord Harris and suggested, 'Time for a sonnet, my friend.'

Whilst Lord Harris shook his head in disagreement, Dr Chettiar asked, 'How about, *Thy write a sonnet. Whilst my love does nothing but fume and fret*?'

'You are such a bastard.' Lord Harris laughed and continued, 'How about I translate a couplet instead for you?

That was the day your love cursed me to death,

When I said, I love you more than my life.'

'No.' Countess Kaur-Hein walked up to them. 'You should replace love with lust, that would better suit Dr Chettiar.'

Dr Chettiar looked at her but Countess Kaur-Hein avoided his gaze.

'I came up to say goodnight,' she said and kissed Lord Harris and HRH Nachiyar. She nodded at Dr Chettiar.

'I shall leave too,' HRH Nachiyar said and kissed Dr Chettiar.

'To tomorrow,' Dr Chettiar poured himself more whisky.

Lord Harris went up to Dr Chettiar and embraced him.

'Tomorrow it is, my friend.' Lord Harris slapped Dr Chettiar's back. He kissed HRH Nachiyar and went to Countess Kaur-Hein. He kissed her and then took something out of his waistcoat pocket.

'Countess Kaur-Hein, I believe this belongs to you.' He placed a ring on her palm.

'It fulfilled its destiny. I wed Joanna with this ring. With this love,' he said.

They departed.

Dr Chettiar remained on the deck. He finished the bottle and opened another one. This time, he did not need a glass. He thought about the race. It was over. He would not be able to arrive at Fort St George without setting foot on British soil because of the Marina Coast. The balloon was to have been his trump card. Now he had nothing. Not even an idea.

This defeat hurt less than being defeated in love.

He had been married when he had met Countess Kaur-Hein. He had been but twelve when he was married to a girl who was ten, and he had met Countess Kaur-Hein, then HRH Kaur, when he was studying medicine in Cambridge.

As you remove your garland to disrobe your pride

What travels to you faster?

My moans in pleasure or my cries in pain.

When she had learnt about his marriage, they had separated.

Dr Chettiar at the present time, gulped whisky as he searched his coat pocket for his wallet, which had that paper clipping. On one side of the clipping was the matrimonial section that had announced the wedding of HRH Kaur to Count Hein and on the other side was the obituary column for Mrs Chettiar who had died from cholera at the age of twenty. Dr Chettiar searched and found a peaceful place to sleep as deeply as death.

Chapter Nineteen

30 August 1907

Day Seventy-One

Lutz House, Madras

Dr Chettiar opened his eyes from his deep slumber. He had slept with his head on the floor and his legs on the frame of a chair. The barrel of an Enfield revolver was pointing at him as he woke up. Mr Pillai fired the revolver and the bullet hit the marble floor right by Dr Chettiar's ear.

'It is easier to kill you than be in love with Lord Harris!' Mr Pillai said as he took off his turban and kurta and metamorphosed into the beautiful HRH Nachiyar with flowing tresses and dressed in a red satin evening gown.

'How late are we?' Dr Chettiar asked as he tried to find something to cover his naked body.

'There isn't anything here I haven't seen in the last 72 days.' HRH Nachiyar smiled as Lord Harris entered. Lord Harris was dressed in a modern type of dinner jacket first introduced in Tuxedo, New York.

Lord Harris raised his hand as if he was about to throw a punch.

'Punch me.' Dr Chettiar went up to him.

'I will do just as you please,' Inspector Davies said and did punch Dr Chettiar. Inspector Davies was dressed in his usual coat.

'But why?' Dr Chettiar rubbed his face as he walked to his wardrobe.

'I have worked out who murdered Governor Roberts,' Inspector Davies announced.

Three pairs of eyes looked at him.

'I have satisfied my intellectual curiosity,' he continued with pride. He walked closer to Dr Chettiar and said, 'But I have decided that it is only just that Mr One Too-Many remains named as the murderer in my report.' He looked at the bruise on Dr Chettiar's face with satisfaction and said, 'That punch was a punishment for attempting to deceive me.'

Dr Chettiar wore a black three-piece suit and accepted a Trichinopoly cigar lit for him by HRH Nachiyar.

As they were ready to leave, Lord Harris offered his arm to HRH Nachiyar.

HRH Nachiyar smiled at him and took his arm.

Dr Chettiar laughed and asked, 'Do you have a sonnet for this situation?'

'The same words that I will recite when you meet Countess Kaur-Hein at this evening's ceremony,' Lord Harris quipped.

'Neither time nor love doth waste nor wait even when I plea,' Dr Chettiar quoted and added, 'Use it in your sonnet.'

As they stepped into a carriage, HRH Nachiyar commented, 'Wouldn't it be fun if you raced each other now to the Madras Cricket Club?'

'No, don't even think it,' said Lord Harris.

The elite of Madras were assembled at the Madras Cricket Club that evening for the announcement of the result from an extraordinary race around the world.

'That is Poongulali, granddaughter of Captain Pandian. She commanded a ship!' a teak merchant remarked as a voluptuous maiden dressed in shimmering green Kancheepuram silk entered. She was accompanied by Pandithurai Thevar. It would be only appropriate to offer condolences as Captain Pandian had died on the way back from Macao.

By the bar, a major in the army remarked, 'But for a tip from Lord Harris, we wouldn't have apprehended that Bose fellow in Yokohama.'

'Well, the news is that Dr Chettiar is friends with that Dr Sun Yat-Sen. Given how Dr Sun Yat-Sen is anti-British, we need to add Dr Chettiar to our list of nationalist fighters and keep an eye on him,' his colleague added.

It was then that HRH Nachiyar arrived accompanied by Inspector Davies.

An aspiring young scriptwriter in the crowd, Ellis Duncan said, 'HRH Nachiyar comes from a lineage of Tamil women who fought tigers barehanded. It isn't a surprise that she drove engines and fought pirates.'

'Isn't that Inspector Davies from Scotland Yard? He was the one who nearly caught that rascal Mr Too-Many,' a sergeant on duty said to his captain.

'It's tragic that Lady Harris died valiantly, having killed that monster,' the captain replied.

'I so feel for Lord Harris. He and the daughter of Governor Roberts would have made a sterling pair.' A buxom memsahib shed tears as her bosom heaved and made her even more vulgar to look at.

'I say, he played the finest ever innings at Lords!'

When the secretary of the Madras Cricket Club said that, the president of the Madras Cricket Club replied, 'Indeed. Did he not thrash Bosanquet?'

Dr Chettiar entered the ballroom along with Lord Harris. The crowd rejoiced and went delirious. Count Hein offered them flutes of champagne. Countess Kaur-Hein, dressed in blue satin with an open back, raised a toast to them.

A bell rang to start formal proceedings and the president of the Madras Cricket Club took to the podium. After the usual introductions of the guests, with stale jokes that only inflated his vanity, he proceeded to the pressing matter of that evening.

'With regards to the clauses, I can confirm that Dr Chettiar did not use any British companies for transportation.'

'Let's just say that he has friends with deep pockets,' a sarcastic voice came from the crowd.

'And friends with deeper hearts!' Lord Harris shouted a befitting reply in support of Dr Chettiar.

'And, yes, both men finished their journey under eighty days,' the president confirmed. He continued, 'Now we arrive at the question of who arrived first at Fort St George.'

The same sarcastic voice shouted again, 'Before that, there is the question of whether Dr Chettiar managed not to set foot on British soil!'

'Do you have a couplet for this situation?' Lord Harris whispered to Dr Chettiar.

'Did I learn?

My mind in lust was then foolish.

And now my heart in love is foolish.' Dr Chettiar was passionate in reciting another of his translations.

Lord Harris looked puzzled at Dr Chettiar.

HRH Nachiyar nudged Lord Harris in the direction of the situation that Dr Chettiar was engrossed in for Dr Chettiar was staring at Countess Kaur-Hein who stood beside him. To be precise, he was staring at her hand that was holding her flute. And to be even more specific, at her index finger, which wore a diamond-in-a-diamond ring, and between the diamonds were dried and fragmented reeds. The remains of his love.

Countess Kaur-Hein turned and found Dr Chettiar gazing at the ring.

She touched his face and said, 'It looks like you are looking for your next adventure.'

'To find my love,' he replied and let her hand stay on his face.

'You need to find yourself,' she said and pulled him close to kiss his cheek.

'I would suggest a race to the top of the world', suggested Lord Harris.

The president announced the winner.

Chapter Twenty

29 August 1907

Day Seventy

St George's Fort, Madras

Thy hurt him.

Rather than wound his love, he would die.

Lord Harris was interrupted from completing a sonnet, as HRH Nachiyar informed him that, 'Dr Chettiar is missing from The Inquilab.'

No one had seen Dr Chettiar since the previous night.

Where could he have gone?

And more importantly, how could he have vanished from the ship? None of the lifeboats seemed to be missing.

'What new trick is that bastard up to?' Lord Harris asked and walked up to the deck.

Inspector Davies and Count Hein were deep in conversation.

Countess Kaur-Hein looked devastated.

'He could not have jumped into the sea,' Inspector Davies asserted.

'If he had to, he would have done so several years ago,' Countess Kaur-Hein said.

Count Hein walked up to his wife and held her close.

Lord Harris paced up and down the deck whilst HRH Nachiyar peered into the horizon.

'It appears that you have won Lord Harris,' Count Hein said as soon as Fort St George was in sight that evening on the Marina Coast of the Bay of Bengal.

Lord Harris looked grim. 'What is the old devil up to!' he exclaimed. He shook his head and added 'What if something terrible has befallen him?'

A rope ladder took down Lord Harris, HRH Nachiyar, and Inspector Davies from the ship, to a boat waiting to carry them to the sandy strip of the coast beyond which was the Fort St George.

An excited Count Hein on The Inquilab ordered, 'Get the cannon ready to fire in celebration of Lord Harris's victory!'

'I will do the honours,' Countess Kaur-Hein offered and took charge of the 8m cannon.

Lord Harris looked around as the boat docked, still unconvinced that he had won. But the cannon fire seemed to confirm his victory.

Countess Kaur-Hein shrieked in horror as she fired the cannon.

When you are away, even the air, hesitates to enter my corpse to decay it.

The friction of your nipples may light my funeral pyre.

Dr Chettiar this time, was not facing the barrel of a gun pointing at him. He was in the turret of the cannon. A womb he had found to sleep in the previous night; a place he had found in defeat. Hence, he was as much bewildered as Countess Kaur-Hein was, in being launched from a cannon.

He had never imagined his arrival at Fort St George coming from being shot from a cannon. He had covered sixty metres of water and sand as he landed inside Fort St George on sacks of sand used for fortification. Sixty metres would remain the world record for a human cannonball flight.

Lord Harris ran into Fort St George. Only on this occasion, it was Dr Chettiar who waited for him ready to throw a punch.

www.ingramcontent.com/pod-product-compliance
Lightning Source LLC
LaVergne TN
LVHW091058150826
845673LV00002B/628

* 9 7 9 8 8 9 2 3 3 9 2 8 5 *